TAKE YOUR BEST SHOT

READ ALL THE BOOKS IN THE

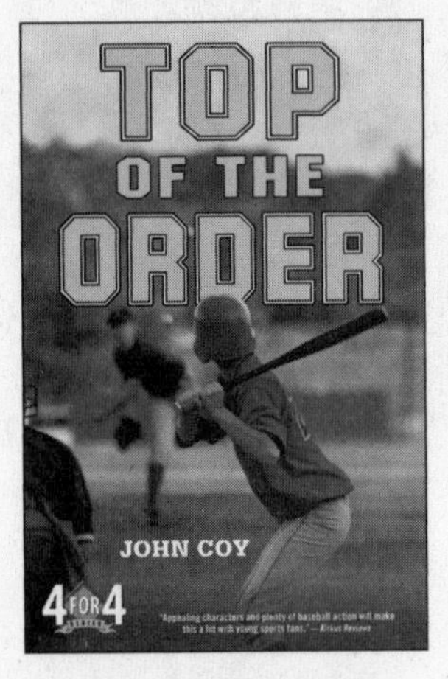

TOP OF THE ORDER

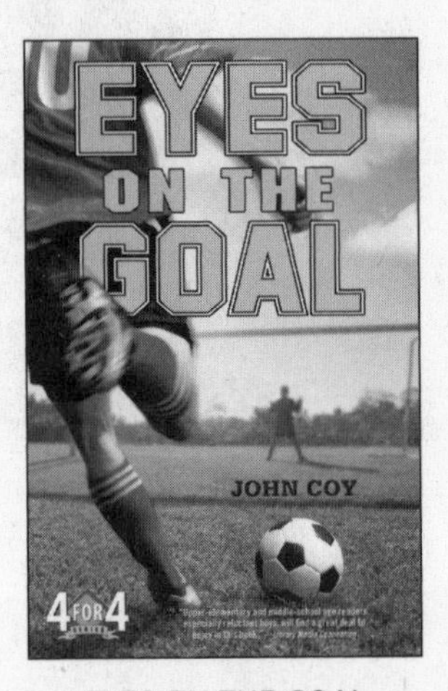

EYES ON THE GOAL

LOVE OF THE GAME

TAKE YOUR BEST SHOT

TAKE YOUR BEST SHOT

JOHN COY

FEIWEL AND FRIENDS
NEW YORK

A Feiwel and Friends Book
An Imprint of Macmillan

 Printed in the United States of America
by R. R. Donnelley & Sons Company, Harrisonburg, Virginia.
For information, address Feiwel and Friends, 175 Fifth Avenue,
New York, N.Y. 10010.

Library of Congress Cataloging-in-Publication Data

Coy, John,
Take your best shot / John Coy. — 1st ed.
p. cm.
Summary: Jackson confronts many challenges in his first year of middle school as his mother plans to get married, the best player on his basketball team leaves, he needs to ask a girl to go to a school dance with him, and his best friend's father is injured in Afghanistan.
[1. Middle schools—Fiction. 2. Schools—Fiction. 3. Basketball—Fiction. 4. Family life—Fiction. 5. Friendship—Fiction.] I. Title.
PZ7.C839455Tak 2012
[Fic]—dc23
2011033584

ISBN: 978-0-312-37332-0 (hardcover)
10 9 8 7 6 5 4 3 2 1

ISBN: 978-1-250-00032-3 (paperback)
10 9 8 7 6 5 4 3 2 1

Book design by Tim Hall

Feiwel and Friends logo designed by Filomena Tuosto

First Edition: 2012

mackids.com

For Liam

TAKE YOUR BEST SHOT

Chapter 1

I'm having a terrible day.

This morning, the bus driver drove off even though he could see me running to catch the bus. I had to ask Dad to give me a ride, and he was angry because he'd been telling me to hurry at breakfast.

In math, Mr. Tedesco gave me detention for talking even though I was only telling my friend Quincy what the assignment was. Tedesco didn't listen to me and threatened to double the detention if I kept protesting.

In the hall, a huge eighth grader slammed into me from behind and called me sixer trash and told me to watch where I was going.

Then, in language arts, Ms. Tremont gave me another detention because I couldn't find my homework and stopped me when I tried to convince her that I must have left it in my locker.

"Homework needs to be here at Longview Middle School, Jackson, not someplace else," she said, and some people laughed.

Now in gym class, Mr. Tieg is making us run three laps around the track and timing us even though it's freezing outside.

"This stinks," I say to Trenton Cromarty.

"Tell me about it."

"No talking," Tieg barks out.

On the other side of the track, Diego Jimenez is in the lead. That's more bad news. Our basketball team, the Jets, has its first game in a week, and we're playing this year on Tuesdays and Saturdays. Diego works on his uncle's roofing crew on Saturdays so he's going to miss half the games.

"Pick up the pace, slackers," Tieg shouts. He's a former Marine who thinks gym should be like boot camp.

I keep plodding around the track. Nothing's going right. Gym was my favorite class back in elementary school when we played games. Now in middle school, it's one of my worst. Tieg said running would warm us up, but he's wrong. I feel so cold my skin might fall off. I might be the first kid ever to get frostbite in gym class in November.

At lunch, my friends and I sit at our table in the back of the cafeteria and practice signing our autographs with black Sharpies for when we're famous. Isaac Wilkins takes a bite of stuffed-crust pizza and a gooey cheese string hangs down his chin.

"Looks like snot," my best friend, Gig, says.

"It's cheese." Isaac grabs it and eats it.

"It's not. It's snot." Gig shakes up his chocolate-milk carton.

"Why are you doing that?" Diego asks.

"It tastes better when it's bubbly, Padre." Gig, whose full name is Spencer Milroy, uses Diego's nickname. He tried to get us all to use nicknames at the start of school, but like a lot of his ideas, nobody else joined in.

Diego and Isaac experiment with different styles on their autographs, but mine all look alike. I turn to Diego. "Is there any way you can play in our games on Saturdays?"

"No way." He puts extra loops on the *z* of Jimenez. "My uncle won't let me miss a day of work."

Mr. Norquist, our assistant principal with the thin moustache, walks by, and Gig lets out a big sigh. Norquist grabs

Cody Bauer and Lance Dahlgren, two big hockey players from the next table, and escorts them down to the office. Gig sighs heavily again.

"What are you doing?" Isaac asks.

"Don't you know, Ike? Norquist's first name is Cy, short for Cyrus." Gig sighs again. "It's funny to sigh every time he goes by."

"You're weird," Isaac says and nobody disagrees.

"Why's your mom here, Julio?" Gig asks me, using my name from Spanish class.

I turn around to look but don't see her.

"Got ya." Gig laughs.

"That's really immature." I put salsa on my taco.

"No, it's not," Gig says. "It's funny."

Quincy Pitman and Dante Lewis, who played football with us, set their trays down.

"Sorry about that detention in math," Quincy says.

"Sorry enough to take it for me?" I bite into my taco.

"Not that sorry," he says.

Dante sits down across from Isaac, two basketball stars at the same table. "We're still looking for another shooter on the traveling team. You should think about it," Dante says.

Isaac shakes his head no.

"Why not?"

"I promised my friends I'd play on the Jets with them."

"But the traveling team is so much better," says Quincy, who was Isaac's favorite receiver in football. "If we had you, we could win the league."

"No." Isaac takes his last bite of pizza. "Diego, Gig, Jackson, and I promised each other that we'd stay together this year."

"But we need you," Dante says.

"We need him more," I say. "With Isaac, nobody's going to beat us."

"Think about it." Quincy opens up his milk.

"I've already decided," Isaac says.

I peel my tangerine and am glad Isaac's being so clear about sticking with our deal to stay together.

In FACS, which stands for family and consumer science, Mrs. Randall is reviewing true or false questions that might be on our quiz. "When finished eating, you should put the silverware on the plate. Raise your hand if you think that's true," she says in her Alabama accent.

Isaac raises his hand and so does my friend Ruby, so I do, too. I watch Ruby, who's got her reddish brown hair pulled back in a ponytail and is wearing a tan sweater that looks good on her. She's drawing on the front of her notebook, which has her name on it in big red letters and three words underneath:

Act . . .
Sing . . .
Love . . .

"That's true," Mrs. Randall says. "Here's another one. A left-handed person should rearrange the settings to the other side."

I raise my hand for false with everybody else. It's not fair to lefties, but lots of things aren't fair.

"Two more," Mrs. Randall says. "True or false? It is acceptable to put your forearms on the table."

Isaac and I both vote false, but Ruby votes true.

"True," Mrs. Randall says. "No elbows on the table, but forearms are okay."

Ruby looks over at me and smiles, and I smile back. No matter how bad the day's going, things feel better when she's around.

"Last one, y'all." Mrs. Randall checks the clock. "It's all right to cut up all your meat at once."

Caleb says something about meat in back, and some kids burst out laughing.

"This isn't funny," Mrs. Randall says. "Etiquette is important. If you do well on the quiz tomorrow, we'll make smoothies. If not, we'll spend the rest of the period reviewing table manners."

The bell rings and we all scramble up.

"False," Mrs. Randall shouts. "Don't cut up all your meat at once."

Isaac and I walk out of FACS together.

"You're not thinking about playing with those guys on the traveling team, are you?"

"Don't worry," he says. "I'm sticking with you."

CHAPTER 2

Ruby walks with me to my locker after FACS.

"What are you doing after school?" She inspects her pink fingernail polish.

"Detention." I pull out my math book.

"Bad luck."

"Yeah, I've got it today *and* tomorrow."

"You've been a bad, bad boy." She shakes her finger at me.

"What are you doing?"

"We've got rehearsal for *The Music Man.* Our first performance is a week from tomorrow."

"What's your part again?"

"I'm Marian Paroo, the River City librarian. I'm getting more nervous as we get closer to showtime."

"You'll do great."

"You're going to come see me, aren't you?"

"Yeah." I pick out another book and slam my locker shut. "We've got our first basketball game a week from today. Can you come?"

"Sorry, I can't." She shakes her head. "We have dress rehearsal." Ruby walks with me to the detention room, which is Mr. Lisicky's, my American studies teacher.

"I'm surprised to see you, Jackson," he says. "What are you in for?"

"Talking and homework." I don't feel like going into it, as I look around at Bauer, Dahlgren, and some of the other troublemakers.

"I hope this is the only time I'll see you all year," he says.

"Actually, I'll be here tomorrow."

"Two detentions in one day. That's bad."

"I know." I pick a table and set my stuff down. "I've got to call my dad to tell him I won't be on the bus and need to be picked up."

"Text him quickly," Mr. Lisicky says. "We don't allow phone calls in here. It's detention after all."

G-Man, my grandpa, picks me up after detention and tells me right away that my dad is upset.

"Where is he?" I ask.

"Taking Quinn to the dentist."

I buckle my seat belt and stare straight ahead.

"What crime did you commit?" G-Man asks.

"I told a friend what the math assignment was and got detention for that. It wasn't fair."

"Detention isn't always fair, but I'm not going to second-guess the teacher," G-Man says. "You should be smart enough to stay out of it." He passes the library, and I realize we're not driving toward his house or ours.

"Where are we going?"

"Today's Election Day. I need to vote."

"How long will that take?" I notice all the candidate signs that feel like they've been up for months.

"Depends how the length of the line is."

"I've got basketball practice tonight. Can't you do it later?"

"No. Remember, I wasn't the one who got detention."

The line stretches out the door at the library, and people are bundled up against the cold.

"I'll stay in the car," I announce. "I've got a book I need to read for school."

"Okay." G-Man climbs out. "Come join me if you feel like it. Elections are interesting. You can come into the booth with me."

I dig my book out of my backpack. G-Man considers lots of odd things interesting.

But after I've read for twenty minutes, I'm ready for something different. I walk downstairs and find G-Man up near the front of the line.

"I'm glad you came in," he says. "I haven't missed an election in over forty years."

Around the basement room, voting booths are lined against the back wall, and up front, people are sitting at long tables. Maybe I can get Mr. Lisicky to give me some extra credit for being here.

"Hi, Marge," G-Man says to a big woman at the registration table. "This is my grandson Jackson."

"Hi, Jackson," Marge says in a warm voice. "I see the resemblance. You look like your grandfather."

"Nah," G-Man says. "He's much better looking. There's only one person he looks like."

"Who?" Marge asks.

I look over at G-Man to see who he'll say.

"Jackson Carter Kennedy. He looks exactly like himself."

"He does," Marge agrees.

"Thanks." I watch G-Man sign his name in a big book. I like that answer. I hate it when adults go on and on about who some kid looks like. Half the time, they're just making it up.

I follow G-Man over to the line where he's given his ballot.

"How do you know who to vote for?" I ask.

"I read the paper, listen to the radio, and talk to people, but on some of the lesser-known offices, like Soil and Water Conservation District Supervisor, I don't know the candidates. Then I see if anybody is Irish or I pick a last name I like."

At the booth, G-Man pulls the curtain aside and ushers me in. He puts his finger to his lips to remind me to be quiet, and I watch as he puts his glasses on and fills in ovals next to the names of candidates.

When he gets to the last race, one for judge, he hands me the pencil and gestures to me to fill it in. I lean forward and see that one candidate's last name is Tomacek and the other is O'Shea.

That's easy. I fill in the circle for O'Shea and G-Man nods. He's right. Voting is kind of fun.

"Let's go over to Sunny's," G-Man says. "It's never too cold for ice cream. Don't tell your dad or Quinn about it, though. You can keep a secret?"

"Yeah."

"We'll get an ice cream to celebrate your first vote. I could go for a cone of Almond Delight."

"I'll get Heath Bar Crunch."

"Did your dad tell you about his new girlfriend?" G-Man unlocks the door to his big Buick.

"No, he's got a girlfriend? What's her name?"

"Something French: Sylvie, Cécile. I can't remember." G-Man rubs his chin. "Don't tell him I told you. He'll tell you when he's ready."

I look at all the people streaming in to vote. Dad's got a new girlfriend. Why doesn't he think we're ready to hear about her?

CHAPTER 3

Dad and Quinn are back from the dentist when I walk into the kitchen, and I can tell from the way Dad stops cutting mushrooms and stares at me that he's angry.

"Two detentions in one day. What's going on?"

"Umm. It was a bad day." I decide not to go into how unfair the detention for talking was. Dad's not going to take my side on it.

"I don't expect one detention, much less two," Dad says.

"What's detention?" Quinn, my seven-year-old brother, comes into the kitchen, carrying a book about dogs.

"Nothing." I can still taste the Heath Bar Crunch in my mouth and remember to keep the secret.

"It's like after-school time-out," Dad says.

"Jackson got a time-out?" Quinn's eyes widen.

"Two of them." Dad pulls a box of spaghetti out of the cupboard.

"What did you do?" Quinn asks excitedly.

"Talking and lost homework." I don't like how excited he is about me screwing up.

"Don't let it happen again," Dad warns. "I don't want you getting another detention all year. Is that clear?"

"Yeah." I want to go to my room and be by myself.

"Do you have homework you need to finish?"

"No, I did it at school."

"All of it?"

"Yeah. That was the only good thing about detention. I got my homework done."

"Have you talked to your mother about this?"

"No, I was going to do it later."

"Do it right now. Let her know what's going on. I don't like you getting in trouble like this when you're here."

I walk into my bedroom and take out my phone. Dad's usually more laid-back, but he doesn't like Mom hearing that I got into trouble when I'm with him. He doesn't want Mom thinking I'm doing worse over here.

—

When I call Mom from my bedroom, she's out with her boyfriend, Ted, to dinner at the White Horse.

"I can call back later."

"No. What is it? I'll go out in the entryway. What's happening?"

I explain about the detention, and just like Dad, she gets mad and tells me she doesn't want it happening again. It's almost like they've talked in advance and agreed upon a joint response.

"We've got parent-teacher conferences on Friday," she says. "This isn't a very good start."

I lie back on my bed and stare up at the ceiling and wait for her lecture to end. It's just a couple of detentions. Mom and Dad act like it's the end of the world.

"No more detention, Jackson. Promise?"

"I promise, Mom."

"Good. I'll pick you up after school on Thursday. I love you."

"Me, too." I click off the phone. No detention means no late assignments, no tardies, no talking in Tedesco's room. I'm going to have to watch it in order to keep my promise.

—

Basketball practice is back at Longview, and it's weird to be at school at night when the classrooms are locked, the lights are off in them, and no teachers are around. The halls feel strange with nobody in them, and I hurry past the one where I saw the ghost with long blond hair on my middle school visit as a fifth grader.

In the gym, Gig's tying his Zig Techs and I sit next to him to put on my black Nikes.

"I got two detentions today and my parents freaked out."

"Two detentions isn't a big deal," he says. "I got four one day last week when I got into arguments with people I didn't even know."

"Didn't your parents get angry?"

"Not really. They pretended to, but Mom's so worried about Dad in Afghanistan that everything else is kind of unimportant. Dad says do my best, but it's hard to focus on school when I'm thinking about him."

"Hey, guys," Isaac says as he and Diego sit down and take off their sweatshirts. Diego's laces are untied, and he kicks off his boots and puts on his New Balance high-tops. Isaac slips out of his black Cons and pulls out a new pair of red Jordans that match our game jerseys.

I look down at the other end of the gym where players from a different team gather. I recognize Cole Gunderson and Steve Stein, who we beat in football. Stein said they'd beat us in basketball, but with Isaac on our team, they've got no chance.

Sam Sportelli, Tony Cerrato, Noah Hauser, and Trenton Cromarty file in. Sam and Tony are both pretty good, but Noah's been hurt in both baseball and football this year, and Trenton's terrible. The only reason he's out is because his mom said he needed to get some exercise instead of reading comics all the time.

Gig tosses me a ball and we walk out to shoot. I position myself on the baseline, my favorite place to shoot. Most people like shooting straight on, but I like being on the side, where it's not so crowded. I aim for the hoop and drain the shot.

"Let's start with some lay-ups," Coach Cerrato, Tony's dad, shouts. He's a big guy with a huge belly. He looks like he'd be out of breath if he ran up and down the court once.

I line up behind Diego and Gig and stretch out my hands. My left thumb, the one I sprained in football, feels fine, but I bend it a few times to loosen it up. When my turn comes, I dribble, shoot off my left foot, and watch the ball bank off the backboard and drop through the net. I love this game.

When I get the rebound, I pass to Isaac, who glides in and flips the ball up. He moves so smoothly and makes it look so easy. He doesn't even look up as the ball drops through the hoop. He knows it's good.

After lay-ups, we form two lines facing each other and practice our chest passes. Gig's my partner, and he puts the pass right on my hands so I hardly have to move them.

"Now, each of you take a step back," Coach says.

Gig takes a big step back and I try to match him. It's harder to get the chest pass there without putting some arc on it.

"Put some force behind your passes, Kennedy," Coach says.

When we split up for four on four, I get to play with Isaac, Diego, and Sam. Tony's guarding me, and I beat him to a rebound.

"Box out, Cerrato," Coach says. It's got to be strange having your dad for a coach and having him call you by your last name.

I pass to Isaac, who fakes a shot at the three-point line. Gig closes out, and Isaac blows by him and banks a shot off the board.

We've got the best player in the league. There's no way we're going to lose.

CHAPTER 4

The next day at school, I concentrate on getting all of my work done and not talking in order to avoid another detention. School's hard enough without worrying all the time about messing up and getting in trouble.

In science, Ms. K. is away on maternity leave because she had a baby girl, and we've got a new long-term sub, Mrs. Browne, who is smiley and enthusiastic.

"Guess what my favorite color is?" she asks.

I look around at the bulletin boards that have been freshly papered in brown and the door that's decorated in brown and have a good idea.

"That's right." She doesn't even wait for an answer. "I love brown."

I've never met anyone whose favorite color is brown, but

I've got a feeling if Mrs. Browne was named Mrs. Turquoise, turquoise would be her favorite color.

"We've got a fascinating experiment today with Life Savers," Mrs. Browne says. "We're going to guess which color will dissolve the quickest in solutions of vinegar and salt water."

Dante raises his hand and says, "I guess brown."

Some kids laugh, but Mrs. Browne ignores them. "I'm sorry, there aren't brown Life Savers. It would be fun if there were. They might taste like root beer or better yet, chocolate."

I look over at the fish tank in the corner, which is more interesting than listening to Mrs. Browne talk about brown. I watch the fish swim around and around and around. What a drag to spend your life trapped like that.

After we split up with our lab partners, I pick green and Dante chooses purple, though neither of us really cares which Life Saver is going to dissolve fastest. We wait and watch them, which is pretty boring, and write down what changes we notice in our notebooks.

As we're observing, Dante asks me about hoops and how our team looks.

"We're going to go undefeated."

"Isaac should be playing with us on the traveling team.

He didn't even try out. If he did, Coach Russell would have picked him."

"It doesn't matter. Isaac's made his decision. He's playing with us."

Dante holds up his hands like he wants me to chill out. I don't like the way he keeps bringing up the issue, like it isn't settled. It is. Isaac's with us.

In American studies, Mr. Lisicky talks about American expansion and conflicts with Native Americans.

"Whenever the settlers desired land, they pressed the government to make treaties to move the tribes farther west. As settlement expanded, new settlers wanted *that* land. They wanted the government to ignore the old treaties and move the Native Americans even farther west."

I draw a picture of a basketball swishing through the net.

"Underneath this tension were fundamental differences about land," Mr. Lisicky says. "For Monday, I want you to write down three differences between the European settlers and the Native Americans on how they viewed land."

I keep drawing basketballs in my notebook. Mr. Lisicky's a good teacher, and I normally like the class, but I can't focus today. I keep thinking about basketball. That's where I'd like to be right now. I even imagine the classroom as a court with a basket behind Mr. Lisicky's head. I look around the class and choose who I'd want on my team and who could be on the other one.

One whole week. I wish we didn't have to wait that long until our first game. I'm ready to play right now.

In FACS, after we've taken and checked our quizzes, Mrs. Randall announces that we did well enough so that we can break into our lab groups and make smoothies.

"Yeah!" We all cheer.

"Y'all did better than I expected," she says. "Now we're going to make a transition. What does the word transition mean?"

"To change," Isaac answers.

"Yes, we're going to transition to food labs, and sometimes y'all don't do that as well as I expect. Go to your groups quickly and quietly."

I'm glad as we move to our kitchen. That's what we like about FACS—making stuff and eating it, not worrying about place settings and table manners.

I gather with my lab partners Ruby, Caleb, and BB. BB stands for Bossy Boots because she always takes control and tells us what to do, but Ruby invented some wild story about how BB is so straight and accurate that it reminded her of a BB gun, and BB believed it, so she lets us call her BB or Double B.

"Who wants to peel and slice the bananas?" Bossy Boots looks down at the green sheet.

I raise my hand. "I'll do it, Double B."

"Wash and slice the strawberries?"

Ruby raises her hand.

"That leaves blueberries and peaches, Caleb," Bossy Boots says. "Blueberries are simple, all you do is wash them."

"That's me," Caleb volunteers.

I stand next to Ruby as she washes the berries. She's got a maroon clip in her hair that matches her top, and her shampoo smells like pineapple.

"I love smoothies," she says. "I'm so glad we did well enough on the quiz so we get to make them."

"Me, too. I got nineteen out of twenty." I slice the bananas on my cutting board.

"Same," Ruby says. "I only missed the question about the placement of the soup spoon."

"That's the same one I missed," I say.

"Here, put everything in the blender now," Bossy Boots

says. She smushes everything in, adds ice, presses the blender buttons, and we watch it all swirl together.

The smoothies taste delicious, and when Mrs. Randall's not looking, I wipe my finger in the bottom of the glass and lick it. I don't think that would be on the quiz as proper smoothie manners, but I want to get every last bit.

As we're walking out of class, Isaac says, "Do you want to hang out at my house after school?"

"I can't. I've got detention." I feel like a complete loser as I say it.

Chapter 5

Friday afternoon, Mom and I enter the gym at Longview for my first middle school parent-teacher conference. Tables are spread out around the gym grouped by subject area, and behind each one, an eager teacher is waiting.

"Last name?" the woman at the sixth-grade registration asks.

Mom nudges me.

"Kennedy," I answer.

"First?"

"Jackson."

"Here you go." She hands Mom a copy of my schedule. "You can go in order, but you don't have to."

"Thanks." Mom studies the schedule. "Let's start with math."

"She said we didn't have to go in order." That's the last place I want to start.

"What's the matter with math?"

"Nothing." I trail behind her as she walks straight to the math section. We take a seat three rows back and wait for the people in front of us.

Behind the table, Mr. Tedesco is frowning and shaking his head at Quincy and his mom. He's probably given him detention for something serious—like breathing. Tedesco, who's got beady eyes and looks like a crow, points to a piece of paper and slides it over for Quincy's mom to see. She doesn't look happy with whatever is on it.

As I watch, I realize that as much as Tedesco likes math, he doesn't really like kids. It's not just me. All kinds of kids bug him.

It's always amazing when people who don't like kids become teachers. Parents are always saying to respect teachers, but they don't realize that some teachers don't respect kids. They don't even like them. Those are the teachers that get all excited when they hand out detentions.

When our turn finally comes, Mr. Tedesco introduces himself to Mom and then puts on his serious face.

"Jackson has potential, Mrs. Kennedy, but he's not living up to it."

"What do you mean?" Mom asks.

"He does okay on tests and quizzes, but he could try harder." Tedesco points to numbers on his printout. "This week he got a detention, and I take major points off for that. Jackson's grade has dropped to a B minus, which is lower than it should be."

I stare at the paper like it will tell me something new, but the same words keep echoing in my head. *He doesn't like kids. He doesn't like kids.*

"Jackson will improve for the rest of the semester," Mom announces like she plans to wave a magic wand and make things be the way she wants them to be. "Isn't that right, Jackson?" She looks at me.

"Uh-huh."

"No more detentions," Tedesco says. "That will help."

Ms. Tremont in language arts gives me a good report and is more encouraging. She looks at me while she talks and explains things. She's an example of a teacher who likes kids. "You've been doing a good job on reading thirty minutes each day out of class," she says. "As you know, that's the minimum expectation. For the rest of the trimester, I'd like you to increase it. Remember you can read anything you like: fiction, nonfiction, magazines, comics, online."

"Really? Online reading counts?" Mom asks.

"As long as it's reading words," Ms. Tremont says.

"Even texting," I say.

"Surely not." Mom shakes her head.

"Texting is reading," I say, and Mom frowns.

"It's reading words and writing," Ms. Tremont explains.

"That's a broader definition of reading than I'm used to," Mom says.

"Yes," Ms. Tremont says. "We want students to get in the habit of reading for pleasure every day. Jackson, I'd like you to increase it to forty minutes a day outside of class. Can you do that?"

I nod. That's the thing with teachers. Even when you do what they want, they want more.

Mom insists on going in the order of my schedule, and the next few go okay. Not great, but none as bad as Tedesco. Señora O'Reilly in Spanish asks me questions in Spanish, which is embarrassing because I'm not very good, and Mom doesn't know Spanish, so she watches me. Señora O'Reilly finally switches to English to say I'm doing okay, but she recommends some extra credit to raise my grade. She hands me a paper and I read it.

Bake Pan de Muerto
Attend a Spanish-speaking church service
Draw a map of Spanish-speaking countries
Interview a Spanish speaker

I reread the last one. I could interview Diego. I look at the details under it.

Write ten questions in Spanish to ask a person who is a native Spanish-speaker. Write down your answers, again in Spanish. DO NOT ask the interviewee to write down the answers for you. Do your own work.

I fold the paper and put it in my pocket, but Mom stops me. "Make sure to do one of those this weekend."

Mrs. Browne, our new long-term sub in science, has of course decorated her table in brown paper, and Mom thinks it's cute. I think it's weird.

"Jackson's a delight to have as a student," she tells Mom,

even though I've only had her a couple of days and I don't think she really knows who I am.

Mom listens closely as Mrs. Browne goes into how exciting science is and how essential a background in science is for any young person no matter what career they choose to pursue.

Mr. Lisicky, my American studies teacher, gets up to greet me and asks who I've brought with me. I introduce Mom, and he tells her I'm doing well in his class.

"Jackson was particularly engaged when we studied the American Revolution." He turns to me. "I expect that same level of engagement now that we're studying westward expansion."

I'm not exactly sure what he means, but suddenly I realize I forgot to do my homework. I can't even remember exactly what it is. I guess he's telling me I need to focus and work harder.

Mrs. Randall, from FACS, saves the day with a big plate of cookies. I take a chocolate-chip one, and it's easy to see why I like her class so much.

"Jackson, you're doing well," she says. "Your tests and quizzes are solid, and you're working well with your lab partners." She checks her notes. "Caleb, Ruby, and Stephanie."

For a second I wonder who Stephanie is, but then I realize it's Bossy Boots. I'm so used to calling her BB or Double B that I forgot her real name.

"Y'all keep up the good work," Mrs. Randall says, and it's easy to see why she's one of the most popular teachers in the school. I'm going to miss her next trimester when I have to switch to industrial tech.

"Your dad will be here in a few minutes." Mom checks her phone while we walk to the door. "He'll drop you off afterward. Remember Heather and Haley are coming this weekend, and tonight we're going to have game night."

Mom says this in an enthusiastic voice, like this is the most exciting news in the world.

"I'll see you in a little while." She steps in for a hug, but I take a quick step back.

She's got to realize she can't be hugging me when tons of kids are around.

Chapter 6

I wait by the front and watch for Dad. I wish he could just ask Mom what everybody said, but he likes meeting all my teachers so he knows who I'm talking about. I can't remember him ever missing a parent-teacher conference. Because Mom and Dad both need to meet my teachers, I've got to go through it twice. Sometimes it's hard to be a kid of divorced parents.

I spot Isaac with his parents at a table on the other side of the gym. They're talking to the advanced-math teacher and everybody is smiling. Isaac gets all A's, so these conferences must be a breeze for him.

Dad comes rushing in and spots me. "Sorry I'm late," he says. "I saw your mom in the parking lot. She said you had a pretty good report but still have room for improvement."

"Uh-huh."

"Where do you want to start?"

"Let's start with Mrs. Randall at FACS. She's got chocolate-chip cookies."

While we're waiting for Mrs. Randall we talk with Isaac and his parents. Mr. Wilkins was my baseball coach last spring, so it's always fun to see him. Isaac's mom is knitting a sweater while she waits.

"Do you want to come over tonight?" Isaac asks.

"Sorry, I've got game night with Heather and Haley."

"Game night?"

"Don't ask." I hold up my hand. "I'll see you at practice tomorrow."

So Dad and I meet everybody I did with Mom. Most of the teachers are cool with it since they've got lots of experience with kids whose folks are divorced, but Mr. Tedesco makes a show of having to go through the printouts in the pile of previously seen students, and Mr. Tieg, the gym teacher, says, "Didn't I see you already?"

Since I've been through it, I know what teachers are going to say, so I pay more attention to how they say it. It's interesting that the teachers I like best, like Mrs. Randall, Ms. Tremont, and Mr. Lisicky, focus more on talking to me, like it's my conference and Dad is observing.

The teachers I don't like as much, like Mr. Tedesco and Mr. Corland in general music, talk more to Dad, like I'm the spectator. Mr. Tedesco goes into the whole detention thing again, but Dad says we've talked about it, and he doesn't expect it to happen again.

After we've finished, Dad says it's good to be able to match names with faces, and he agrees that Mrs. Browne decorating everything in brown is a bit much. "Good thing she's not named Mrs. Pink or Mrs. Aqua."

As we're walking out, Ruby is coming in with her parents. She zips right up to us and starts making introductions.

Ruby's mom has the same reddish brown hair as she does and stands tall, but her dad is short and bald and seems kind of shy. It's clear who Ruby takes after.

"How are rehearsals going?" I ask.

"We've got a million things to do," Ruby says dramatically. "We've got dress rehearsal tomorrow night and twice next week and student matinees on Wednesday, Thursday, and Friday and public performances Friday and Saturday, and I still don't see how we're going to be ready. It might be a total disaster."

"Ruby's exaggerating." Her mom pats her on the shoulder. "They're going to do fine. Every production we've ever seen at Longview has been first-rate. That's not going to change."

Her dad and my dad are standing around looking awkward, so we say our good-byes.

"You're coming to the show next Friday, right?" Ruby asks.

"Yes, definitely. I'll be there."

That night, after we've finished our Chinese food, Mom hands out scorecards and pencils for Yahtzee in the living room. Ted, her boyfriend, sits between his daughters, Heather and Haley, on one side of the coffee table, and Quinn and I sit next to Mom on the other.

Quinn, who's a math nut, loves Yahtzee and explains to Haley how to keep score. "It's important to get your bonus on top, and you've got to average three of each number to do that."

"This feels so cozy having everybody together," Mom says.

"Sure does," Ted says.

I don't say anything since I'd rather be over at Isaac's.

Heather, who's in the same grade I am but goes to Twin

Park, had high roll so she starts. She rattles the dice in the cup and shakes a three, a five, a two, a four, and a one.

"That's a bad roll," she says. "I don't have a single pair."

"That's an excellent roll." Quinn points at her scorecard. "That's a large straight. Forty points."

"Thanks." Heather marks it down and Quinn grins.

"This is so much fun," Mom says.

Quinn's a lucky Yahtzee player, but I'm still surprised when he gets five sixes on his third roll. "Yahtzee!" he screams.

But then Haley gets a Yahtzee and so does Ted. Mom gets a small straight and rolls a six to turn it into a large straight. Everybody is having good luck except me. I have to take my chance—the one where you total up the dice when you've got absolutely nothing else—way too early.

Haley gets another Yahtzee and looks around like she can't believe how easy the game is. That's beginner's luck.

Mom's helping Ted, who says he hasn't played since he was a kid, and he's having a good game, too. He's got more than enough for his bonus on top and still has his chance box unfilled.

I wish I had another chance, a second chance. I've always thought it would be good if the scorecard had two chances.

After a dozen turns, everybody has enough for bonus except Heather and me. I'm way short, and she's got four on her twos, six on her threes, and nothing yet for her fives.

Quinn looks over at her scorecard and announces, "Heather doesn't have much on top."

Mom turns to Ted, and I watch Heather, who's blushing. She's thin with a flat chest, but that's not what Quinn meant. Mom shakes her head at Quinn.

"What?" he asks.

"Heather's doing fine." Mom pats her on the leg. "She's going to get four fives. You watch."

Heather looks down as the dice spill onto the table.

"There's one five," Mom says.

Heather shakes again.

"There's the second one," Ted says.

Heather shakes the cup super long and the dice rattle. She rolls them out and lucks out with two more fives.

"She got it!" Mom yells.

When we total the scores, everybody earns the bonus except me. Haley wins, but Quinn's right behind, and everybody has a good score. Everybody but me.

"Great game," Mom says. "Now I have something even better."

"What could be better than Yahtzee?" Quinn asks.

"This." Mom holds up her hand and a diamond ring that I hadn't noticed before flashes on her finger. "Ted and I are getting married."

Chapter 7

"What?" The word pops out of my mouth.

"We're getting married." Mom reaches for Ted's hand and gazes into his eyes like they're in a movie.

"Congratulations." Heather gets up and hugs Mom and then her dad.

"Can I see the ring again?" Haley leans close to Mom, who turns her hand so the diamond sparkles.

"Can I be in the wedding?" Quinn asks.

"Yes, of course," Mom says. "We're just going to have a small ceremony of family and friends."

Ted's looking at me like I should say something.

"Congratulations." I shake his hand.

"Thanks, Jackson." He acts like I'm giving him some kind of permission.

The announcement came so fast that I'm unsure what to

think. We're living in his house, so it shouldn't be a complete surprise, but it still caught me off guard.

"When's the wedding?" Heather asks.

"Two weeks from tomorrow. We wanted to do it soon," Mom says.

"I'll need a new dress," Heather says.

"We'll get you and Haley dresses," Ted says.

"The wedding's on a Saturday?" I ask.

"Yes. Saturday afternoon," Mom says.

"I've got basketball on Saturday afternoons." I can't believe she could forget that.

"A wedding is more important than basketball practice," Heather says.

"It's not practice. It's a game. We've got games on Saturday. I can't miss a game."

"What time's your game?" Ted asks.

"I don't know. I'll have to check the schedule."

"The wedding is at four thirty," Mom says. "Your games are usually over by then, aren't they?"

"Yeah." I still can't believe she'd pick a time without checking with me first. Mom's looking at Ted and holding his hand.

I should go over and say congratulations to her, but I don't feel like it. She should have remembered my game.

"Are you going to keep your name or take Dad's?" Heather asks.

"I'm going to be a Torgerson like you." Mom smiles.

I pick the Yahtzee dice off the table and shake them in the cup. Mom's switching everything. Even when she and Dad got divorced, she kept Kennedy. Now she'll have a different last name than Quinn and me. I roll the dice but nothing matches.

After a few more games of Yahtzee, Mom announces it's time for apple pie, ice cream, and hot cider. She goes through to the kitchen with Ted, Haley, and Quinn. Heather and I are left to pick up the scorecards and pencils and put them in the box.

"It's kind of fast," I say to Heather, who'll now become my stepsister.

"Your mom's not PG, is she?"

"What?"

"Pregnant," she whispers.

"No. I don't think so." Mom hasn't said anything, but then she didn't warn me in advance about the wedding.

"I thought it might be yours, mine, and ours."

"What?"

"My dad has me and Haley, your mom has you and Quinn. Maybe they'll want a baby together."

"No." I hadn't even thought about Mom having a baby with Ted. I don't like thinking about that at all.

At practice Saturday morning, we're running off screens, catching passes, and taking shots. I brush by Diego, catch the ball from Gig, and shoot. The ball hits the back of the rim and bounces off.

"Get your feet set before you shoot, Kennedy," Coach Cerrato says. "Don't rush the shot."

We run this drill over and over, but Isaac is the only one who consistently knocks down his shot.

"Let's work on your off-hand now," Coach says. "How many of you are right-handed?"

We all raise our hands.

"Okay, I want you to start out on this side of the basket." He points to a spot outside the line. "Then drive across in front and shoot a hook shot with your left hand."

Gig starts and puts up a soft shot that rolls around the rim and falls off. Diego's left hand isn't bad, probably because he's a switch-hitter in baseball. Coach passes the ball to me, and I concentrate on dribbling. I plant my right foot and toss up a left-handed shot. It banks off the board but hits the side of the rim and falls off.

I throw the ball back to Isaac, who glides across and flips a left-handed hook in off the board like it's the simplest shot in basketball. He's better with his left hand than some of the guys on the team are with their right.

Afterward, Coach splits us up into teams for a four-on-four scrimmage. I'm with Gig, Sam, and Tony. Isaac's with Diego, but he's also got to play with Trenton and Noah, who aren't very good. Coach is trying to balance the sides to make it as fair as possible.

Gig dribbles the ball and bounce passes to Tony, who finds Sam cutting to the basket. Diego reaches back to block the shot, and Isaac picks up the loose ball and races the other way. He passes to Trenton, who quickly passes it back, and Isaac drains a long jumper.

Gig brings the ball upcourt and passes to me on the wing. I look for Tony or Sam, but neither is open. I pass back to Gig, who drives and then kicks the ball back out to me. I've got an open shot, but it's a little farther out than my range. I dribble twice and pass to Sam.

"When you've got an open shot, take it," Coach calls out.

Sam puts up a runner that bounces off the rim, and Diego grabs the rebound. He hasn't played that much basketball, but he's a good rebounder and defender—and he's big and strong. That makes a huge difference under the basket.

Gig rips a steal from Noah and beats everybody to the hoop for a layup. His speed is a plus on the court, and he handles the ball well.

Isaac brings the ball up and passes to Noah, who sends the ball right back since he doesn't want Gig to steal it again. Isaac flips the ball to Trenton, who takes one bounce and passes it back. Isaac bounces the ball at the top of the key, and Diego muscles under the basket to rebound.

Everybody on their team wants Isaac to shoot, and they know if he does, it's got a good chance to go in. I double-team him with Tony, but he splits us and drives to the hoop.

Isaac's impossible to guard, and I'm glad that once the real games begin, he's on our team. Then the rest of the league will have to try to figure out a way to stop him.

Mom's made me tomato soup and a grilled-cheese sandwich for lunch since I'm starving after practice.

"Where's everybody?" I ask.

"Ted took Heather and Haley to look at dresses, and Quinn went, too. He thought he might get a Matchbox car out of the deal."

"Mom, can I ask you something?"

"Sure." She turns from the sink and dries her hands.

"You're not pregnant, are you?"

"No, of course not. Are you saying I've put on weight?" She puts her hands on her stomach and pulls it in.

"No, no." I set my sandwich down. "I wondered with the wedding announcement."

"No, Jackson. Ted and I have been talking about this since we moved in, and once we decided, we thought it made sense to do it before the holidays when everything gets so hectic."

"So you're not planning on a baby?"

"No. Ted and I are very happy with our two girls and two boys." She comes over to the table and puts her hand on my shoulder. "We've got the perfect family."

I dip my sandwich in the soup and take a bite of gooey cheese. I'm glad Mom's not pregnant, but I don't like the perfect-family talk. We're not going to be the perfect family.

Chapter 8

Sunday afternoon, Dad picks us up, and I wonder about the best way to tell him the news.

"Mom's getting married to Ted," Quinn blurts out.

"I know," Dad says. "She called, and I gave her my congratulations. I'm happy that she's happy."

I look out at the outlines of trees against the blue sky as we drive to the Y.

"How you guys doing?" Dad asks.

"I'm going to be in the wedding," Quinn says. "I get to be the ring bearer."

"Jackson?" Dad looks over at me.

"It's fine."

"You're sure?"

"Yeah, it's kind of sudden."

"It is, but your mom said they've been talking about it for a while and decided to do it before Thanksgiving."

I keep staring out the window in the bright sunlight, thinking about what it's going to mean to have Ted as my stepfather. Dad seems okay with it, but he doesn't have to live with Ted. He's not the one who's got to go to a wedding in two weeks on the same day as a basketball game.

G-Man joins us at the whirlpool, and as usual he's wearing his green-and-yellow floral surfer trunks. We've tried to tell him a million times that they don't look good on him, but he insists we don't know what we're talking about.

"Look, they've opened up the rope." Quinn points.

At the end of the pool, a lifeguard stands, holding a fat rope with a knot on the bottom. She hands it to a chubby kid who swings out over the water, holding onto it, lets go, then drops in with a big splash.

"Let's go," Quinn says.

"I'm ready," G-Man says. "Jackson?"

"I'll be down in a little bit."

"Me, too," Dad says.

I drop down into the bubbles of the hot tub and let the jets blast away at my back.

"Okay?" Dad asks.

"Yeah. It feels like a lot's changing."

"It is," Dad says. "It's going to take a while to catch up with it, but Quinn's doing fine. I'm fine. You concentrate on taking care of yourself and let me know if there's anything you need. Got it?"

"Yeah." I nod. I wouldn't be able to talk like this with Ted. There are certain conversations you can only have with your dad.

"Come on, let's go jump off the rope." Dad stands.

"Okay." As we walk down, I watch G-Man grab his knees for a cannonball.

"Nice one." The pretty lifeguard gives him a thumbs-up.

"I want to try that," Quinn says.

"Jackson first," G-Man calls.

I take the rope from the guard, swing out over the water, and let go. I blow bubbles under water and try to let everything that's happening wash off me.

Señora O'Reilly didn't say what questions to ask in the interview for extra credit, and she didn't say it had to be done in person, so I call Diego Sunday night. I'm sure she's hoping for insights into Mexican culture, but I ask Diego in Spanish about his favorite sports. Soccer's number one, of course, and baseball is number two, but for three, he chooses football, which surprises me because he never played on a team before this fall. I ask why he likes it, and he says because you get to tackle people, which is the same reason I love it. Basketball is number four, but he's pretty good at that, too.

It's fun to talk to him in Spanish even though my Spanish is super-basic. I ask him where he was born (San Antonio, Texas) and his favorite food (his mom's chicken enchiladas) and what he wants to be when he grows up. He says he wants to be a professional soccer player, but then he surprises me by saying if that doesn't work out, he wants to own a *panaderia*, a Mexican bakery, and when I ask why a *panaderia*, he says because he likes the smell of fresh baked bread and cookies. He also says that he wants to go to college and be the first person in his family to graduate.

"*Muchas gracias*," I say since we're past ten questions. I'm glad I was able to talk to him in Spanish, and I'm glad to have my extra credit.

Monday at lunch, I sit with my friends, and Gig's complaining about the amount of homework we get. He's wearing an old shirt that looks like it's about ready for the trash.

"Teachers keep piling it on," he says.

"They give you time in class," Isaac says.

"I don't get enough time." Gig eats a chicken nugget. "I've got a ton of work in Spanish. Señora O'Reilly's a hard teacher."

"Spanish is easy." Diego takes a gulp of milk.

"For you. You speak Spanish. It's no fair that you get to take Spanish when you already know it."

"You know English and you get to take English."

"It's not English. It's language arts."

"Same thing." Diego bites into his cheeseburger.

"What's the deal with your shirt, Gig?" I ask.

"Norquist is making me wear it inside out because he says the message on it is inappropriate."

"What's it say?" Diego asks.

Gig pulls it up and slides closer to me. I know it says I'M WITH STUPID and the arrow points toward me.

I give him a shove even though I know it's his favorite shirt.

"Norquist said the shirt is a form of bullying." Gig sighs loudly and pulls it back down.

What about Wolfram and Steck, the two eighth graders from my bus? Why doesn't Norquist do something about the real bullies around here?

"Did you sigh while he was talking to you?" I ask.

"Yeah, and the whole time I was changing my shirt I sighed heavily."

"Are you guys going to the dance?" Isaac dips a chicken nugget in barbeque sauce.

"What dance?" Diego asks.

"The school dance in two weeks," Isaac says. "Everybody dresses up and has fun. It's going to be great."

"Who are you going with?" I ask.

"I'm going to ask Vanessa who's in FACS with us."

"They're going to have prizes for best dancer, best couple, best outfits," Gig says. "I heard they had some outstanding prizes like an iPad and a PS3. I'd like to win one of those."

"Who are you going to ask?"

"I've got lots of options," he says. "I've got to choose."

"So you are going?" I'm kind of surprised.

"Yeah, I'm going to win one of those prizes."

"What about you, Diego?" Isaac asks.

"I want to go," he says.

"Jackson?"

"I'm thinking about it." I didn't know everybody else was going. If they weren't, it would have been easy for me not to go. But if all of them go, I want to go, too. I don't want to be the only one not going like I'm some kind of loser.

"We've got READ Club tomorrow in the library," Isaac says. "Don't forget to bring a bag lunch."

"Mr. Amodt said we were going to do some kind of fun project later this month, but he didn't say what it was." Gig crushes up his empty fruit cup.

Diego, Isaac, and Gig speculate about what it might be, but that's not what I'm focused on. I'm thinking about the dance. It's not easy for me to ask a girl to something like that, but I know who I want to ask. I think she'll say yes, but there's a part of me that's not sure. That's the part that makes it hard.

Still, I know what I need to do.

Chapter 9

I'm looking out the window in American studies, thinking about our first basketball game tomorrow night. I can't wait to get on the court and get our first win, but I'm also still thinking about the dance and Ruby.

I'll see her next period in FACS, and maybe I can ask her then. I'm not sure if I should talk about the dance and how much fun it's going to be and then ask her or if I should just come straight to the point.

"What's another difference?" Mr. Lisicky looks around the room and zooms in on me even though I don't have my hand in the air. "Jackson."

"What?"

"Do you understand the question?"

"No." I shake my head.

"This was the homework from Friday. I need you to be more engaged, remember?"

I nod.

"What's another difference between how European settlers viewed land and the way that Native Americans did?" Mr. Lisicky asks.

I'm relieved when he calls on somebody else who answers that the settlers believed in private property and owning a piece of land, while the Native Americans believed land was a gift from the creator for everybody to use.

"Yes, what else?" Mr. Lisicky asks.

Another smart girl raises her hand and talks about Manifest Destiny and how the settlers believed it was God's plan for them to drive the Native Americans from the land because they were Christians and the Native Americans were not.

"Yes," Mr. Lisicky says. "Throughout history, people have used religion to justify all kinds of behavior. What's another difference?"

"Some settlers believed that the Native Americans weren't using the land properly. They were hunting by following the buffalo, and the settlers believed it was better to have cows and pigs and raise crops."

"Yes. Very good," Mr. Lisicky says.

I try to keep paying attention, to stay engaged, but I keep thinking of Ruby. I keep picturing her smiling face and wondering if she'll say yes.

In FACS, we all take our seats, and I don't have a chance to say anything to Ruby since she's talking with Vanessa. Mrs. Randall starts lecturing about the proper way to load a dishwasher even though this seems like one of the simplest things in the world—just jam the dirty dishes in.

But of course she insists that there is a correct way to load dishes to "ensure maximum efficiency and cleanliness." If FACS were like this all the time, it would be super-boring. Making things and eating them is what makes it fun. And part of the reason that's fun is because Ruby's in my lab group.

I look at her across the room sitting up straight and taking notes. She's wearing a light blue Abercrombie zip-up sweatshirt and tight jeans, and like everything she wears they look good on her. Suddenly, she turns and sees me looking and smiles. It's like she can read my thoughts. I smile back, and even though we're on opposite sides of the classroom, we're connected.

Mrs. Randall passes out a work sheet with a diagram of a dishwasher on one side of the page and listings of different plates, bowls, cups, glasses, and silverware on the other. "Y'all match the items with where they should go in the dishwasher."

I examine the diagram and realize I should have been paying attention and taking notes while she was talking, rather than staring at Ruby.

When the bell rings to end FACS, Isaac's talking to Vanessa, the girl he said he was going to ask to the dance. Maybe he's doing that right now.

I watch Ruby and wait until she's close to the door so we can walk out together.

"How'd you do on the dishwasher work sheet?" I ask.

"Fifteen out of fifteen. It was easy. How'd you do?"

"Not so good. Eight out of fifteen. As long as the stuff gets clean, what does it matter?"

Ruby laughs, and I think about how to bring up the subject of the dance. Here's my chance. I'm with Ruby by myself. I smooth my hair down and hope my ears don't look too big.

"Hey, Marian," someone shouts from behind us, and Ruby turns around.

"Marian?" I ask.

"I'm Marian in *The Music Man*. We're all calling each other by our play names today." Ruby unzips her sweatshirt halfway to show off a white top underneath. I know the dress-code rules about how low the neck of a shirt can be, but girls get around it by wearing low-cut tops and zipping up when teachers are around.

The guy who shouted hurries up, and I can tell he's older. He's taller, broader in the shoulders, and has dark hair and eyelashes.

"Ready for rehearsal, Marian?" He ignores me and talks directly to Ruby.

"I'm nervous," she says.

"You're doing super." He takes both her hands and looks at her like I'm not even there. "When you got the part I wasn't sure a sixth grader could handle the female lead, but you're fantastic."

I keep staring at the guy's eyelashes. They look like he's used something to make them longer and darker.

"Uh umm." I clear my throat.

"Oh." Ruby turns to me. "Do the two of you know each other?"

"I don't think so."

"Definitely not," Eyelashes says.

"Jackson, this is my friend Chaz. Chaz, this is Jackson."

We shake hands, but neither one of us is interested in the other. Ruby called him a friend. I know they're in the play together and actors are dramatic, but he's still holding her hands and telling her how fantastic she's doing, and that feels a bit over-the-top.

"We've got to go," she finally says. "Rehearsal time."

"See you tomorrow." I hold my hand up and watch the two of them go down the hall together. Chaz? What kind of a stupid name is that?

CHAPTER 10

Tuesday morning, Gig's sister Sydney comes over to my table in homeroom, and since the bell hasn't rung yet, we end up talking.

"How's basketball going?" She's wearing jeans and a faded Hollister shirt.

"We've got our first game tonight. We're going to be great."

"Gig says you won't lose a game."

"He's right."

"That sounds dangerous to be so confident." She brushes her brown hair behind her ear.

"It's not dangerous if we back it up. Isaac's the best player in the league. Nobody's going to beat us." I pull my NBA notebook out. "How's your team?"

"I think we can be good. We've got our first game tomorrow afternoon."

"Good luck."

"Yeah, you, too."

"Hey, Sydney, how's your dad?"

"Okay. I talked with him this weekend. It's still strange that it's morning here when it's night in Afghanistan."

"Gig hasn't said anything lately. He doesn't seem to want to talk about it."

"I know," she says. "We're doing a presentation for the Veterans Day assembly this afternoon, and he threatened not to participate. Everybody else from the Military Kids groups is doing it, and finally Ms. Monihan persuaded him by saying it was a way of honoring all the people in uniform. He doesn't like calling attention to it."

"Why?"

"I don't know. Why don't you ask him?"

"I don't think he wants to talk about it."

"It doesn't hurt to ask," Sydney says. "I'll see you in READ Club at lunch."

"Oh, shoot. I forgot to bring a bag lunch."

"I brought an extra sandwich and chips in case someone forgot. You can have it."

"Thanks. That's awesome." The bell rings and she goes back to her seat.

I'd never think to bring an extra sandwich and chips for someone who forgot. I can't even remember to bring my own lunch.

At READ Club, Gig, Isaac, Diego, and I take a table in back. Sydney swings by and drops off the sandwich and Garden Salsa SunChips.

"Hey, what's up with that?" Gig asks as she drifts away. He's a year older than Sydney, but they're in the same class because he got held back a year in kindergarten.

"I forgot my lunch and she brought extra."

"Cool," Diego says.

"She's trying to impress Mr. Amodt," Gig says. "She always tries to suck up to teachers."

I bite into the cheese sandwich and it tastes great. I don't agree with Gig about Sydney, but there's no point in arguing with him.

"Did you losers ask anybody to the dance?" Isaac sets his apple, potato chips, and peanut butter sandwich out in front of him.

"I did," Diego says.

"You did?" I pick up a piece of cheese that's fallen on the table.

"Yeah, I'm going with Gabriella from Spanish class. Melody, I mean. Gabriella's her Spanish-class name."

"She said yes?"

"Yeah." Diego hits my shoulder. "You act like you can't believe it."

"No." I hold up my hand, but I am surprised. Diego asked someone and she said yes. He makes it seem so easy.

"What about you, Gig?" Isaac asks.

"Still narrowing down the field, Ike." Gig unscrews the cap on his Gatorade.

"We've got a lot of new books for you today," Mr. Amodt announces. He's got short black hair and thick sideburns. "Publishers sent me a bunch of ARCs for their spring books. ARC stands for advance reader's copy, and you can read them before any other students in the country do. I put them out on the tables with the other books. After you've finished eating, you can browse the tables."

"How many ARCs can we take?" Sydney asks.

"As many as you can read. Bring them back next time like you would a regular book." Mr. Amodt gestures around at the tables filled with books. "I've got too many books in here. They're not supposed to be here. They're supposed to be at home with you."

I take another bite of the SunChips. I don't ever choose them, but they're pretty good. I'm glad Sydney brought an extra lunch so I don't have to starve. I'm also glad that everything I read for Mr. Amodt counts for my daily reading with Ms. Tremont. I like it when I can double dip.

"In two weeks, we'll have a special READ Club." Mr. Amodt puts his glasses in his pocket. "I guarantee you will enjoy it. Sometimes in order to learn how something's put together, you've got to take it apart."

The Veterans Day assembly is the last period of the day, and the whole school is packed into the gym for it. We file in by our last-period classes, so I get to sit next to Isaac and Ruby.

Onstage, the principal, the counselors, and three veterans from the VFW are all introduced, and then Assistant Principal Norquist gives a speech. He talks about how the end of the First World War, the armistice, took place on November 11, 1918, at eleven in the morning, and that's why we still celebrate Veterans Day on November 11.

He says how important it is to honor everybody who has worn a uniform and served in the armed forces and that we must always remember those who have given the ultimate sacrifice—their lives—to protect the freedom that we enjoy today.

The whole time he's talking, I'm watching Gig and Sydney and the group of students who are seated at the back of the stage. Sydney's concentrating on what Norquist is saying, but Gig's looking around and tapping his feet like he'd rather be anywhere else. He's not even sighing with Norquist standing right in front of him.

When Norquist finishes his speech, which goes on way too long, Ms. Monihan, one of the counselors, takes the stage. "We have students here at Longview who have fathers, mothers, brothers, sisters, or other relatives serving in the military. I want them to come up to the front of the stage now, and I want you to give them a big round of applause to show how much you appreciate the sacrifice they are making."

Sydney stands up right away, but Gig hangs back and is one of the last students to move to the front of the stage.

Everybody in the audience stands and cheers loudly and most of the students onstage smile. Not Gig. He looks down and rubs the back of his neck like he can't wait for it to end.

Chapter 11

Thump, thump, thump. I bounce the basketball at the free throw line before our first game against the Rams. I aim for the hoop and make my shot. I slide over one spot and Gig moves to the line. He bounces the ball and makes his free throw. Diego bounces the ball tentatively and pushes up a shot, and we're all surprised when that goes in.

"Way to go, Diego," I say.

"Keep it going." Coach Cerrato claps.

Isaac is next and he knocks his shot down. Tony steps to the line, takes a breath, flips the ball in his hands, and makes his shot.

Five in a row. I knew we'd be great.

The next shooter is Trenton, and he dribbles the ball like he's pounding it into the floor. He takes aim at the hoop and throws with all his strength, but the shot is way off. Air ball.

"Good try," Coach says. "Start a new streak."

Sam makes his shot, Noah misses, and then it's back to me.

"Knock it down," Isaac says.

I bounce the ball three times, eye the hoop, and hope the ball goes in. I shoot, but as soon as it leaves my hands I know it's off. The ball bangs against the side of the rim, bounces off the board, and Isaac jumps to grab the rebound. Sometimes I get too nervous when everybody is watching and I think too much about the shot. I just need to relax and shoot.

Gig makes his shot and then the ref blows his whistle. I pick up the loose ball and we all stand around Coach.

"Everybody plays at least two quarters," he says, "so when it's your turn to sit, know you'll be going back in at the quarter break."

I wipe my face with the sleeve of my red jersey.

"Here's the starting lineup." Coach checks his notepad. "Hauser, Milroy, Wilkins, Jimenez, and Cromarty."

I'm disappointed not to be starting, especially since Gig, Isaac, and Diego are.

"Jets, on three." Coach sticks his hand out, and we put ours on top. "One, two, three."

"Jets!" we shout.

"Protect the basketball," Coach says. "Get off to a good start."

All the starters shake hands with the person guarding them, and Diego positions himself for the opening tip. The ref throws up the ball, and Diego taps it to Isaac, who flips it to Gig.

Gig holds up his index finger to call out play number one, and Diego sets a solid screen that frees Isaac. Gig passes the ball, and Isaac catches and shoots. Two to nothing.

"Way to go," I shout.

"Good movement," Coach claps.

On defense, Gig steals the ball from his guy and tosses it to Isaac on the break. Isaac passes it back, and Gig flies in for a layup. Four to nothing.

The whole first quarter is like that. We keep getting easy hoops, and the Rams look confused, like they don't know what hit them. When the quarter ends, we're up twelve to two, and Isaac scored eight of our points.

"Good start, good start," Coach says. "Kennedy, Sportelli, and Cerrato, check in to play with Milroy and Jimenez."

I wipe my shoes on the wet paper towels that Coach put on the floor for traction. I'm glad to be going in but disappointed not to be playing with Isaac. He's sitting out with Noah and Trenton, the two worst players. Maybe that's part of Coach's strategy to let them play with Isaac since he's so good.

I start the quarter underneath the basket and size up my guy, number four, who's my height but heavier. The pass goes into him, and he sends it back out. He tries to back me down, but I slide around him to block the passing lane.

A shot goes up from the free throw line, and Diego muscles the rebound down. He passes to Gig, who brings the ball up. Gig calls out play number three, and Diego sets a screen that Gig slides off. He passes to Tony, who doesn't have an open shot, so he passes to Sam.

We dribble and pass the ball around without taking a shot. We're all so used to getting the ball to Isaac that we're not exactly sure what to do when he's on the bench.

"Look for your shot," Coach calls out, and finally Gig puts up an off-balanced runner that rims out. The Rams rebound and work it around on offense.

"Screen," I call as number four sets up behind Diego under the hoop. Diego turns to see him and slides past.

Number four drives to the hoop, but I hold my ground, and he gets whistled for the charge.

"Foul on number four, Orange." The ref signals to the scoring table. "Red ball."

Sam passes the ball to Gig, who races upcourt. He finds Diego, who's wide open under the hoop. He bounces it off the board for two.

Diego's better than I thought. He's strong on defense and a good rebounder, and when he gets the ball near the hoop, he puts in the shot. We're going to be even better than I expected.

At halftime, we're ahead twenty to six, and I've got three points on a rebound basket and one free throw. As we run our layup drill, I look over at the chairs. Dad and Quinn are sitting together, and Dad's showing Quinn something on his iPhone.

Behind them, Quincy and Dante have come in. I'd like to believe they're here to cheer us on, but that's not what I think. They're here to see how well Isaac does and to try to persuade him to join the traveling team.

The second half is a blowout. Isaac goes into a zone and can't miss, and we keep feeding him the ball. The final score is forty-seven to sixteen, and Isaac totals twenty-five points in three quarters of play. He scored more points by himself than the Rams did as a team. He also had more than everybody else on our team combined.

We slap hands with the other team and then gather around Coach.

"Nice first game," he says. "We've got room to improve, but it's good to get that first win."

I watch him as he talks. I'm glad we won, too, but I would have liked to play more. I only played two quarters and ended up with just three points. Tony got to play three quarters even though I'm better than he is. Maybe that's because his dad is the coach.

Quincy and Dante corner Isaac as he's changing his shoes, and I slide over to hear what they're saying.

"You were on fire!" Quincy slaps his hand.

"This league's too small for you," Dante says. "You need to step up to the next level for some decent competition."

"No, I'm good," Isaac says.

"Too good," Quincy says. "You need to play with some real ballers."

I walk over to Isaac and slap his hand. "Good game."

"You, too," he says. "Way to fight for those rebounds."

“We’re not done with this,” Dante says as he and Quincy leave.

I’m glad to see them go. I want them to understand that Isaac’s not going anywhere.

CHAPTER 12

The next morning, while I wait for Gig at his locker, Lance Dahlgren, Kenny Clark, and Cody Bauer strut by in their hockey jerseys like they're the toughest kids in the school. Clark's a little guy who looks even smaller when he's sandwiched between Bauer and Dahlgren. He looks more like a basketball point guard than a hockey player.

"Good game last night," I say to Gig when he finally shows up.

"The Rams suck," Gig says. "We've got Speros and the Bucks on Saturday. They're a lot better."

"And we're not going to have Diego because he's got to work for his uncle."

"You're going to have to handle Speros." Gig spins his combination.

"I need more minutes. I only played two quarters last night."

"You'll play more on Saturday." Gig opens his locker.

I shift my books from one arm to the other. "What did you think of that assembly yesterday?"

"Stupid," Gig says.

"Why?"

"I don't like it when they make a big deal out of things," Gig says. "I told Ms. Monihan that I didn't want to do it, but she said it was important to the group that I participate."

"Why didn't you want to?"

"I don't like calling attention to what my dad's doing. He doesn't either. He says it's his job, part of signing up for the National Guard. I just want him to finish his tour and come back. Drawing attention to it makes me nervous. It feels like it increases the chances of something bad happening."

I stand and listen. I can't imagine what Gig's going through with his dad in Afghanistan.

"Maybe it sounds crazy," he says, "but that's the way I feel."

"No, it's not crazy."

He gets his books out of his locker and I wait. I wish we

had a class together, but we don't all day. Instead, we separate and head in opposite directions.

School's settled into a predictable routine of classes. Ms. Constantine is fine in homeroom. Tedesco's terrible in math, and his room is too hot and stuffy, but I've been careful not to talk and to get all my work done so I don't get another detention. Ms. Tremont is good, but she expects a ton of reading. Corland is Mr. Boring, the most boring teacher ever. Tieg's strict in gym. Then I have lunch with Gig, Isaac, and Diego, the best part of the day.

Advisory with Ms. Marcus gives me a chance to do some of my homework. Señora O'Reilly's nice for Spanish, but she gives too much homework. Mrs. Browne in science is goofy, but she doesn't really know what's going on, so we don't have to do that much. Mr. Lisicky is good, but he expects a lot, and then finally I go to FACS, where I see Ruby and Isaac and we get to eat our work.

Anything that comes up to break the routine is great, and today the afternoon periods are all shortened for the sixth-grade matinee performance of *The Music Man*. I walk with Isaac into the theater, and we agree that Veterans Day assembly yesterday and *The Music Man* today is excellent since it means less class time.

When the lights dim and the curtain opens, *The Music Man* begins with a group of guys sitting in a train. They've got on fake mustaches and old-time hats, but I recognize one eighth grader from my bus and another sixth grader from math.

They break into song, and I can't imagine singing and acting in front of all the sixth graders. We've been warned by Mr. Norquist to be on our best behavior, and Mrs. Randall's sitting behind us, watching our every move.

Back onstage, the train arrives in River City, and a man picks up his suitcase and says he's going to give Iowa a try. His name, Professor Harold Hill, is on his suitcase, and he's the one that the men have been saying is a con man.

I watch him as he moves around the stage. He's the guy Ruby introduced me to: Chaz. He's convincing as the con man persuading people to believe things that he's making up.

And then Ruby comes onstage as Marian Paroo, the librarian. She looks older with her reading glasses and her hair pulled back in a bun. She's kind and trusting, as she is in real life, and a part of me wants to run up onstage and warn her about Professor Harold Hill, who we know is a liar.

When Ruby sings, I'm stunned. I had no idea she had such a beautiful voice. It's the best singing I've ever heard from a sixth grader, and it's obvious why she got the main part over everybody else in the school.

I've never been a fan of musicals, but I get pulled in watching Ruby. Marian is nice to Amaryllis, the girl she gives piano lessons to, and sweet to her younger brother Winthrop, who's shy and doesn't like to talk.

Chaz is a strong singer, too, especially when he leads "Seventy-Six Trombones," but I'm surprised the people in River City believe Harold and fall for his scam. I don't like it when Chaz has scenes with Ruby, and I particularly dislike it when he sings "Marian the Librarian" and dances with her and says, "I love you madly." When he tries to kiss her, I'm glad she takes a swing to slap him, but unfortunately, he ducks, and she hits someone else.

At the end of the first act, the curtain closes, and the audience cheers. Most sixth graders are probably like me. They couldn't imagine being up on a stage and doing that in front of people for a million dollars. But I can tell Ruby loves it. She's totally into the character of Marian, and she's so convincing that we believe she is a librarian who also teaches piano lessons.

I think back to the one-act play I saw her in a couple of months ago in which she played Gwendolyn. She's totally different now. She's created another character.

"Ruby's excellent." Isaac leans over to me.

"Yeah."

"I didn't know she could sing."

"Me either."

"She could be on *American Idol.*"

As the curtain opens for Act Two, I'm nervous. I'm worried about Marian falling for Harold Hill. But I'm also worried about Ruby. I'm worried about her and Chaz. I'm worried about how much he likes her and whether it's all acting or if some of it's real.

I'm also worried about how much Ruby is into plays and musicals and what a star she is and how little I know about any of that. It seems like a foreign land with different rules.

In the second act, Marian has more scenes with Harold, and she falls for him even though she knows he's dishonest.

I can't follow everything that's going on and get confused when Ruby—Marian—kisses some guy named Charlie, who sells anvils and is played by another good-looking eighth grader.

Marian gets more and more sucked into Harold's scheme, though she should be smart enough to see through him, and I'm crushed when the show ends with Marian in Harold's arms—Ruby in Chaz's arms. That's the worst ending possible.

Chapter 13

After dinner, I sit down at the computer in the living room to do some research for American studies. Mr. Lisicky wants us to find out about the events leading up to the Battle of Little Bighorn, but he didn't say how far back to go. I'm clicking back and forth between websites, but most of them are about the battle and General Custer leading the U.S. Seventh Cavalry.

I'm glad to be interrupted when my phone rings, but I'm not quite as excited to see it's Mom.

"Hey, Jackson, how are you doing?"

"Fine."

"Do you have your white dress shirt and your good shoes there?"

"I don't know. Why?"

"I want you to see if they fit. I've got my wedding prep list in front of me, and I want to make sure you and Quinn have everything you need."

"When is it again?"

"When is it? A week from Saturday. I can't believe you haven't written that down."

"Yeah."

"Go to your room right now and check on that shirt and shoes and try them on. See if they still fit and call me back."

"Okay." I shuffle off to my room and try to decide which is worse: trying on a dress shirt or doing homework.

I flip through the shirts in my closet and find the white one. When I take it off the hanger, it already looks too small. I can't remember the last time I wore it as I pull my sweatshirt over my head.

I try on the shirt and the sleeves are way too short, and it's tight in the shoulders. I take it off and hang it back in my closet and find the dress shoes in back. I try to push my feet into them, but they're too small, too. I kick them off, throw them back in the closet, and call Mom.

"They're both too small."

"I thought they might be. You've grown a lot this year."

"Yeah." Growing is one of those strange things. Nothing

changes day by day, but then you try something on and realize you've changed a lot.

"Ted's offered to take you and Quinn shopping this Saturday to get everything you need."

"Mom, I've got a game on Saturday."

"Yes, I know. He thought you could go after it or before it, whatever works better."

"I'll think about it." Going shopping with Ted and Quinn doesn't sound like a fun thing to do on my weekend.

"Jackson, this is a generous offer on Ted's part. Decide what time works best and let me know by Friday."

"Okay."

"How's school going?"

"Okay. I've got homework tonight."

"Did you do that extra-credit homework for Spanish?"

"Yeah."

"Good. I've got to go. Someone else is calling. Give Quinn a hug from me. Love you."

I turn off my phone and go back to the computer. I'm not going to go find Quinn right now and give him a hug.

A few minutes later, I'm interrupted by another call, and this time it's Gig.

"Going with a star dancer," he says.

"What are you talking about?"

"I asked Zoe Croyden to the dance, and she said yes. She does gymnastics, and she's the best dancer in the sixth grade. We're going to win one of those prizes for sure."

"Great."

"Have you asked anybody yet?"

"No."

"What are you waiting for?"

"I don't know." Isaac, Diego, and Gig are all going to the dance, and I haven't even asked Ruby. I try to go back to my homework about Sitting Bull, Crazy Horse, and Custer, but I can't get Ruby out of my mind. Ruby and Chaz. Every time I picture her, I see that hug with Chaz.

"Dad, can we read this book?" Quinn wanders into the living room.

"Sure. What's it about?"

"Different kinds of dogs."

"I should have guessed," Dad says.

"Can we get a dog? Maybe for Christmas?"

"Quinn, we've been through this. Who'd take care of the dog when you and Jackson are at your mom's and I'm working?"

"Maybe we could have someone come in, like a dog walker."

"We're not going to hire dog walkers. I know how much you love dogs, but it's just not practical."

Thinking about asking Ruby out reminds me about G-Man saying Dad was going out with someone. "Who are you dating?" I ask.

"Simone, a woman who works at another restaurant. We've only gone out a couple of times. If it turns into something more, you'll meet her."

"But I love dogs," Quinn says.

"Mom said to say hi, Quinn."

"I wish she weren't allergic so we could have one there." He sticks out his lower lip.

"What's Simone like?" I ask.

"She's smart, interesting, and funny." Dad pats the couch. "Come on over here, Quinn. Let's read that book together."

While Dad and Quinn are doing that, I take my phone and go back to my bedroom. I scroll through my past calls looking for Ruby's name. She'd called me a few weeks ago about some homework in FACS. I should have asked her about the dance then. I find her name and want to press her number, but I'm not quite ready. I sit down on the bed, stand up, walk to the window, go back to the bed, and sit down.

Instead I phone somebody else—Isaac.

"Hey, what's up?" he says.

"Not much. Trying to do some homework." I get up and walk around the room.

"Me, too. You asked anyone to the dance yet?"

"No, but I'm going to call someone tonight."

"Who?" he asks.

"Ruby from FACS."

"The star of the play today?"

"Yeah." I stare out at the bare trees.

"You better get on it fast. She's going to have a hundred guys asking her after playing that hot librarian."

"Yeah."

"Call her up, talk about the play, then ask her."

"Yeah, I will."

"Right now," he says.

"Okay. Bye."

I've got to do it. I stare at my phone hoping it will ring and it will be Ruby, and she'll say how much she's looking forward to going to the dance with me. But it doesn't work that way. I've got to ask. That seems totally unfair. Why do guys have to ask? Why do they have to risk being rejected?

My thumb hovers above my phone, and I can't prolong it any longer. I press the button and the call goes through.

"Hello."

"Hi, Ruby. It's me. Jackson . . . from school . . . from FACS."

"Hi, Jackson," she says cheerfully.

"You were great in the play today. I couldn't take my eyes off you."

"Thanks."

"Everybody's saying you were the best."

"The whole cast is terrific. Our rehearsals were mixed up this week, and I didn't think we'd be ready, but everybody pulled it together." Ruby talks about a couple of technical things that went wrong with the lighting, and I'm not sure how I'm supposed to go from talking about the play to asking about the dance. I thought when I said I couldn't take my eyes off her, she'd get a hint, but she breezed right past that. Finally, she stops talking and I push ahead.

"The school dance is coming up a week from Friday," I say.

"Yeah, I'm looking forward to it."

"Are you going with someone?"

"Yeah, Chaz asked me yesterday. His full name is Charles Robert Simmons, Junior. Isn't that a fantastic name? He's so talented, and I was so surprised that he'd want to go with a sixth grader. He could go with any girl in the school." Ruby goes on and on about Chaz and what a great performer he is and how he wants to act professionally.

I want to puke. By the time I was ready to ask her, it was too late.

Chapter 14

I pull up the hood of my sweatshirt as I climb the hill to the bus stop. It's cold this morning with an overcast sky, and it's getting darker as we move into mid-November. The dark makes it a lot harder to get up for school.

"Did you ask Ruby?" Isaac asks when I get to the stop.

"She's already going with somebody."

"Who?"

"Professor Harold Hill." I kick a rock and it skids down the street.

"Who?"

"Chaz. That slimy guy from the play."

"I told you all kinds of guys were going to ask her."

"Yeah." Asking Ruby earlier wouldn't have made any difference. She might have still said no. Maybe she would have waited for somebody better to ask. Or even worse, she might have said yes, and then changed her mind when Chaz asked. That would have been worse.

"No big deal," Isaac says. "Ask someone else."

It is a big deal. I wanted to go with Ruby, and I thought she liked me. But she's a good actor. Maybe she was acting all that time in FACS when we were lab partners or maybe she's like that to all kinds of guys.

When the bus comes, Isaac and I grab our usual seat in the middle. In back, Wolfram, the eighth grader who wears sunglasses, and Steck, the one with spiked hair, are arguing and swearing. That's one new thing I've learned in middle school: loads of new swear words.

The checked-out bus driver doesn't say anything to them like usual. He keeps listening to his bad music and driving.

"Think fast, Sixer," Wolfram says.

Something slaps against the back of my head. I reach back and get a hand full of gooey cream.

"Direct hit!" Steck shouts.

"It's a Twinkie." Isaac reaches into his pack and rips a piece of paper out of his notebook.

I try to wipe it out of my hair but worry that I'm going to smell like Twinkie for the rest of the day.

—

At my locker, I grab my books. Amanda, my locker neighbor, spins her combination.

“Hi, Jackson.”

“Hey.” I've gotten used to being down here with the seventh graders. Some of them don't even realize I'm a sixth grader who's only down here because my old locker broke.

“How you doing?”

“Okay.” I want to tell her about Ruby, but it would sound too stupid—like some little sixth-grade drama.

Amanda bumps a water bottle off her shelf, but I move quickly to catch it before it hits the ground.

“Good hands,” she says as I give it back. “Thanks.”

“Are you? Are you going to the dance next week?” I try to ask casually.

“Yeah. You?”

“I'm thinking about it.” I smell like Twinkie. Just like I feared.

“You [illegible]hould go. It's fun.”

“Is [illegible]ie going?”

“[illegible] she's going with an eighth grader. Why are you ask[illegible]

[illegible]ondering.”

“Were you going to ask her if she wasn’t going with anybody?”

“No, no.” I hold up my hands.

“I don’t believe you,” Amanda calls as I head down the hall.

A few days ago, it seemed like hardly anybody had been asked to the dance. Now it seems like everybody has. A window was open for a short time, and I missed it completely.

As I come around the corner, I spot Wolfram and Steck, the bullies from our bus. I turn around and hurry the other way before they can see me. I don’t need any more Twinkies or something worse. One bad turn or one moment of not paying attention can result in disaster. Last week, Trenton walked into the wrong bathroom, and Wolfram and Steck gave him the choice between a chocolate swirlie or eating a piece of pizza that had been face down on the bathroom floor. Trenton picked the pizza.

“What were the events leading up to the Battle [illegible]f Little Bighorn or Battle of the Greasy Grass as the Nati[illegible]meri-cans called it?” Mr. Lisicky asks in American stud[illegible]

A few kids raise their hands, but Mr. Lisicky ofte[illegible] on people who don't have their hands up, so this doesn't mean we're safe.

One girl talks about Custer coming out from Fort Abraham Lincoln near what is now Bismarck, North Dakota, and another boy talks about Major Reno and Captain Benteen, but I can tell from Lisicky's face, he's frustrated by their answers.

"What I'm asking," he paces back and forth in front of the class, "is what events caused these two sides to go to war?"

A smart girl raises her hand and says they were fighting about land.

"Be more specific," Lisicky says.

She shrugs her shoulders, and he turns to me. "Jackson."

"I think it had something to do with the Black Hills."

"Yes, finally," Lisicky says. "What about the Black Hills?" He keeps looking at me.

"The settlers wanted them."

"Be more specific. Anybody?" Mr. Lisicky wanders up and down the aisle like he's looking for a lost dog. "Sixth graders, we need to do better than this."

He moves back to the front of the room and points to a spot on the map. "Little Bighorn or Greasy Grass wasn't an isolated incident. It was part of a much larger picture. For tomorrow, I want you to do a better job of researching this. What events led to this battle? I'll give you a hint. Many of the Lakota, Arapaho, and Northern Cheyenne warriors knew General Custer. What did they know about him? What was the outcome of the battle? And what were the aftereffects?"

That sounds like a lot of work. I listen to Lisicky talk about the location of the battle and watch as he brings up pictures from the Internet on the Smart Board of a prairie landscape with snowcapped mountains in the distance.

"This is the land they were fighting over," Mr. Lisicky says. "If this was your land and someone tried to take it, would you fight for it?"

At basketball practice Coach Cerrato has us running a three-man weave, and Gig's practicing his dance steps as we wait in line.

"Sharp passes," Coach says. "As soon as you catch it, pass it."

I pass to Isaac and then race to the right side. Isaac passes to Diego, who passes to me. I flip the ball back to Isaac, who lays it in off the board.

"We're going to work tonight on less dribbling," Coach

says. "Jimenez, Kennedy, Hauser, when you get a rebound underneath, put the shot up. No dribbling. Don't pass the ball out. Go right back up."

I bend over and tighten the laces on my Nikes into a double knot.

"Speros is the main force for the Bucks," Coach says. "I want him to work on defense and pick up some fouls, so we want you post players grabbing offensive rebounds and shooting."

Coach sets up a drill where we pair up, and he shoots from outside. On the miss, we each go after the rebound.

"Offensive players, as soon as you get the ball, put it back up."

I'm matched against Diego, and he pushes me out of the way when the shot goes up. He grabs the rebound and puts in the layup.

"That's the way, Jimenez," Coach claps. "Kennedy, don't let him dominate you like that."

That's easy for him to say, but Diego's a lot bigger than me.

When we switch places and I'm on offense, I get a rebound and instinctively think of passing it back out to Isaac, but Coach wants me to go right back up, so I put up a shot, but Diego blocks it.

"Go strong," Coach says.

Diego wipes his face on his jersey. He's playing well tonight, and we could use him on Saturday against Speros, who's even bigger than he is. It sucks that he's got to work for his uncle.

I'm going to be stuck with Speros on my own.

CHAPTER 15

Friday morning the halls are packed, and I focus on the girls. Who's going to the dance? Who'd like to go but hasn't been asked? Who'd say yes to me?

I'd envisioned going with Ruby and having a great time. Now, I've got to think of somebody else to ask, and I've got to do it soon since the dance is in a week. But asking Ruby was tough enough. What's it going to be like to ask someone else?

Gig's not at his locker, which is unusual because he always waits until the last possible second before going to homeroom. Maybe he's with Zoe, that star dancer, practicing his moves.

In homeroom, Sydney's absent, too. That's weird. Gig didn't say anything at practice last night about missing school today or them doing anything this weekend. Besides, we've got a game tomorrow afternoon. Gig wouldn't miss a game.

At lunch, I ask Isaac, Diego, Quincy, and Dante, but none of them have seen Gig or heard from him today. He didn't say anything to any of them about not being here either. I rip open my potato chips and notice my hands shaking.

In advisory, Kelsey, who's Sydney's best friend, is standing by her table before the bell rings.

"Have you heard from Sydney?" I ask.

"No, she's not in school. I don't know what's up."

"Did she say anything yesterday?"

"No. It's not like her. I'm worried."

"Me, too."

We take our seats after the bell, and Ms. Marcus hands out announcements about Science Club, and then we work on our homework.

I've got math as usual because Tedesco likes to load on the work. As I'm doing it, I try to come up with a good explanation. Maybe Gig and Sydney skipped school to do something with their mom. Maybe it's Mrs. Milroy's birthday and they're having a special family celebration. But nothing is convincing or makes much sense.

I watch Kelsey on the other side of the room as she does her homework. She's got new blue fingernail polish on and a silver ring on her little finger that sparkles. She's out for basketball and is pretty. I've always gotten along fine with her. I could ask her.

Maybe she'll think it's strange if I ask her since we haven't been hanging out or doing anything special. But maybe she's as desperate as I am to have somebody to go with.

I try to focus on my homework, but it's hard with all the other stuff going through my mind.

When the bell rings, I go over to Kelsey's table and walk out with her.

"Are you going to the dance?" I try to sound like it's no big deal.

"Yeah," Kelsey says excitedly. "Sam Sportelli asked me yesterday. What about you?"

"Still thinking about it," I say. It's beginning to feel like everybody is taken.

"You should go."

"Let me know if you hear anything from Sydney, okay?"

"I will. Let me know if you hear from Gig."

So Kelsey and I exchange phone numbers, not for the usual reason, but for something I hope isn't as bad as I fear.

—

"What led up to Little Bighorn?" Mr. Lisicky asks in American studies, and this time I'm ready, so I raise my hand, but Mr. Lisicky calls on somebody else.

"The Native Americans thought the Black Hills were sacred and off-limits to white settlement," a girl says.

"Why did they think this? Jackson?"

"They'd signed a treaty with the United States."

"Yes, the Fort Laramie Treaty of 1851," Lisicky says. "This provided sixty million acres of the Black Hills 'for the absolute and undisturbed use and occupancy of the Sioux.' And how long was this treaty supposed to last?"

I raise my hand again because I wrote this down.

"Jackson."

"For as long as the river flows and the eagle flies."

"Exactly." Lisicky chops down with his right hand. "That's a long time. But did that treaty last?"

"No," another girl says. "The government renegotiated the treaty seventeen years later and reduced the amount of land to twenty million acres."

"Yes, the Fort Laramie Treaty of 1868 granted the Black Hills to the Native Americans, but did that last?" Lisicky says.

"No, because gold was discovered in the Black Hills," another kid answers.

"And who led the expedition into the Black Hills and brought prospectors with him to search for gold?"

I wave my arm excitedly.

"Jackson?"

"General George Armstrong Custer."

"Custer led the 1874 expedition that found gold, and even though the treaties were very clear that the Black Hills belonged to the Native Americans and were off-limits to white settlement, prospectors poured in hoping to strike it rich."

"That was unfair," one girl says.

"It was illegal," someone else says.

"Yes," Mr. Lisicky says. "The Native Americans had an agreement with the United States, and the United States broke it. This is what led to the events of June of 1876, the battle we know as Little Bighorn, in which General Custer and the entire Seventh Cavalry were killed by warriors under the leadership of Gall, Crazy Horse, and Sitting Bull."

I listen as Mr. Lisicky describes the battle, but my thoughts drift back to Gig. Where is he? What's going on?

"For Monday," Mr. Lisicky says, "find out when this dispute about the Black Hills ended."

Great. I hate it when I get homework for over the weekend.

—

At the end of school, I walk down to the counselors' office. I'm hoping Ms. Monihan, Gig's counselor, is around and that she knows something.

When I walk in, she's talking with Mr. Price, the other counselor, so I take the chair outside her office and wait. I send a text to Gig, since school is officially over, but he doesn't text back.

Ms. Monihan finishes up her conversation with Mr. Price and opens her door.

"Hi." I stand up. "I'm Jackson Kennedy."

"How can I help you, Jackson?"

"I'm a friend of Gig's. I mean Spencer Milroy's. Do you know where he is?"

"Gig didn't come to school today."

"I know. Do you know what's going on?"

"I'm not allowed to talk about other students because of confidentiality requirements." She forces a tight-lipped smile, and I can tell she knows something that she's not telling me.

When I get to the car, Mom's talking about wedding plans and getting me a new shirt and shoes with Ted, but I hold up my hand.

"Mom, Gig wasn't in school today. Neither was Sydney."

"Maybe they're both sick. There's a lot going around."

"Mom, I want to go over there right now. Let's check. If everything is fine, we can do wedding stuff."

"Really, do you think that's necessary?"

"Yes."

"You're not overreacting?"

"No, Mom. I need to do this."

"Okay," she says. "We'll go over there, but I'm sure everything is okay."

Chapter 16

When I ring the bell at Gig's house, nobody answers. I press it again, but nobody comes. I look back at the car, where Mom's on her phone. I put my ear to the door and think I hear something inside. I pound on the door and hear footsteps.

Mrs. Milroy cracks open the door and peeks out. Her face is a mask of dried tears.

"Is everything okay?"

She looks like she's about to start crying. I stand there, not sure if I should stay or go.

"Is Gig here?"

She nods.

"What happened?" I ask.

She wipes her eyes with her palms.

"Is Gig's dad, I mean your husband, okay?"

She shakes her head no and starts to cry.

"Who is it?" Sydney opens the door, and I step into the entry. Her mom climbs the stairs, and I look at Sydney, whose face is all red.

"I'm sorry," I say.

"My dad's in intensive care. An IED, an Improvised Explosive Device, hit his truck and blew it up. We don't know how he's doing."

"I'm so sorry." I feel close to tearing up.

"Thanks," she says.

"Can I see Gig?"

"He doesn't want to see anyone or talk to anyone right now," she says.

"I know, but maybe I should go talk to him."

"I don't think that's a good idea," she says. "He wants to be left alone."

"Okay, let me know as soon as you hear more. Let me know what I can do."

"I will." Sydney's trying so hard to be brave and strong. I open my arms, and she steps forward, and I hold on tight for her and for Gig, my best friend, who I can't even see.

In the car, I tell Mom what happened and she's horrified. "What do you want to do?" she asks.

"I want to go home and be by myself."

She doesn't protest or try to talk me out of it. "I'm so sorry, Jackson," she says.

"I know." The tears flow and now it feels okay to let them.

At home, I sit in my room and stare out the window waiting for news. Nothing comes, and I try to guess if not hearing something is better or worse. I remember Gig at the Veterans Day ceremony and how uncomfortable he was having all that attention paid to him because his dad was in Afghanistan.

I take out my phone and call him, but he doesn't answer, so I send a text.

Later, Mom brings me down some pepperoni pizza and a root beer.

"Any news?" she asks.

"No."

"Do you want to come out and join us or do you want to stay here?"

"Stay here." Being in my room by myself makes me feel closer to Gig.

"Okay."

I call Dad to tell him the news, but there's nothing he can say that will make it feel better. There's nothing anybody can say.

I wish there was something I could do. Anything. I wish there was something to make it all go away.

Saturday afternoon, we've got a basketball game, and it feels so insignificant, so unnecessary. We should cancel it until we hear about Mr. Milroy.

But the game goes on, and I run the layup line after I tell Isaac and Coach Cerrato about what's happened. I look down at the other end where Nick Speros is shooting from the baseline. I played football with him a couple of months ago, but last spring, he was a real jerk to Sydney when she played baseball with us.

Coach starts Isaac, Sam, Tony, Noah, and me. Since we don't have Diego, I've got to jump against Speros for the tip. We shake hands, but he doesn't seem very friendly.

The ref tosses the ball, and Speros controls it easily. I run back on defense, and right away, Speros lowers his shoulder and bumps me.

"Basketball, not football." I push him back and get whistled for the foul.

"Play smart, Kennedy," Coach calls out.

Without Gig and Diego, we only have six, so I need to stay out here. Without me, Speros would clean up. I try my best to box him out and keep him off the boards, but he's a beast. The refs are letting things go, and he's crashing around chasing after every loose ball. On offense, Isaac's missing more shots than usual, as if his mind is somewhere else.

Speros establishes position and calls for the ball from Trey, whose number, three, matches his name. But when Speros slams back against me, I slide out of the way, and he loses his balance and gets called for traveling.

"Good play." Isaac slaps my hand.

He hits a three pointer right before the halftime buzzer to put us up twenty-three to twenty-one.

"Kennedy, try fronting Speros a bit this half." Coach scratches his belly. "On offense, get the ball to Wilkins. Let him take over."

When I walk to the drinking fountain, I think about Gig.

I walk over to my bag and check my phone, but there's no message from Sydney.

The second half goes by in a blur. I switch to playing in front of Speros to make it harder for him to get the ball. I get extra motivation thinking about what a jerk he was to Sydney.

In the fourth quarter, he beats me to the hoop, but I chase after and swipe at the ball. I time it perfectly and thwack the ball out of bounds.

"Yeah," I say and feel like I got one for Sydney.

"Great block." Isaac slaps my hand.

On offense, I get two layups but miss two free throws. Isaac's shots finally start dropping, and he keeps us in the lead.

Late in the fourth period, after Isaac's fouled on a drive, I notice Dante and Quincy cheering. They're with a tall black man, and he's leaning in and talking to Isaac's dad.

Isaac looks over at them and then dribbles the ball three times at the free throw line and drains the shot. We're up by two. Isaac's second shot is too strong, and the ball bounces up. I roll away from Speros and get a hand on it, but knock it out of bounds.

"Defense," Coach shouts. "Hands up."

Trey dribbles at the top of the key and looks for Speros,

who's calling for the ball. I shade to the left of him, and when the pass comes in, I time it perfectly. I tap it out to Isaac, who beats everybody down court for the layup.

We're up by four and close it out.

After the game, Isaac talks with his dad and the traveling-team coach. I check my phone again, but there's still no news from Sydney.

Mom and Ted come up to congratulate me, but then they start talking about wedding shopping. Sam walks off the court, and I think about him going to the dance with Kelsey.

The dance is six days away, and everybody I know is going. I'm not going with Ruby. I'm not going with anybody.

Chapter 17

I stare at the colors in front of me, and I lose focus.

"Since it's a November wedding, I suggest fall colors like these browns and tans. These combinations produce some subtle but lovely variations."

The colors blur into those of the desert, the landscape Gig's dad was driving in right before the bomb went off.

"I like this." Ted holds up a tie. "It will go well with my suit. Jackson, Quinn, and I could all wear the same ties. That would look sharp."

"I agree," the salesman says. "Ties can be the unifying element that pulls everything together."

My vision is locked on the colors in front of me like I'm in a trance. I imagine the noise of the truck engines the moment before the blast.

"Here are a couple more," the salesman says. "Each of these has a touch of red."

"No red," I say loudly. I see a line of blood in the sand. "No blood." I hold up my hands as though I'm under arrest, and the salesman steps back and looks at me like I'm crazy.

"We don't need red." Ted hands the ties back to the salesman and glances at me to see if I'm okay.

I'm not. I'm waiting to find out if Gig's dad is going to live or die, and here I am looking at ties like that matters. It's the last place in the world I want to be, even though nothing I do will make any difference for Mr. Milroy.

"Here are a couple of other nice browns." The salesman is not giving up. "A hint of orange here."

"No brown, no tan, no orange," I say.

"What colors do you want, Jackson?" Ted says.

"I want green," I say. Green, the color of growing things. "Green with some blue." Blue, the color of water, colors that remind me of life.

The salesman picks up the brown and tan ties and takes them away. Ted looks at me as though I've lost my mind, but he doesn't know what to do.

I should tell him why I don't want those colors, but I don't feel like it. I don't feel like shopping for ties and talking about a wedding or doing anything until I know whether Gig's dad is alive or dead.

When I get home, I call Gig again, but he doesn't answer. I haven't heard anything from Sydney either. She said she'd call when they got news. Maybe she forgot. I could call their home number or go by the house again, but I don't want to disturb them if they haven't heard.

My phone rings and I jump. But it's not Gig or Sydney. It's Isaac.

"Have you heard from Gig?" he says.

"No."

"Me either. Hey, why don't you come over tonight?"

"I don't know." I remember Isaac talking with Dante and Quincy and the traveling-team coach. Why isn't he doing something with them?

"We'll order pizza and watch movies."

"I don't know."

"Come on, Jackson. It's better to wait together."

"Okay."

"Good," Isaac says quickly, and I wonder if something else, other than waiting together, is going on.

Isaac and I sit in his living room as he orders a large meat lover's pizza to be delivered. Isaac's mom is a knitter and a half-finished sweater sits out on a table. Tall bookshelves packed with books line the wall, more books than at Mom's and Dad's combined. Isaac's older sister Renee searches around for her house keys.

She's tall and beautiful, and a hint of perfume trails her as she checks her hair in the mirror in the front hall. As someone who doesn't have an older sister, I find the process girls go through to get ready mysterious.

"Don't invite any more guests to your party," she says.

"It's not a party." Isaac waves me into the kitchen.

"And don't make a mess," Renee calls out and whooshes out the door to meet a guy who's waiting for her in the drive-way.

Isaac opens a bag of Flamin' Hot Cheetos and hands it to me. "Have you asked anyone else to the dance?"

"Nah." I sit down at the counter and grab a napkin.

"What are you waiting for? It's less than a week away." He pops open a root beer and slides it over to me.

"I don't know if I'll go."

"Why?"

"I don't know." I take a long gulp.

"Just ask someone."

Isaac doesn't realize that it's not that easy for me. He's got all kinds of girls who'd go with him in a second. If someone said no, he'd ask someone else. But I was counting on Ruby. Now I don't know who to ask.

"It's going to be fun," Isaac says.

I reach for some more Hot Cheetos and watch Isaac looking at me. I look back at him crunching up his can.

"What?" he says.

"You've decided."

"What?"

"You're going to join the traveling team. Quincy and Dante got to you, didn't they?"

"No, that's not it."

"No, you're not joining the traveling team?"

"No. Yes. I mean no, that's not the reason." He shakes his head in frustration. "I am joining the traveling team."

I wipe my fingers on the napkin and feel angry.

"It wasn't Quincy and Dante. I already told them no. It was my dad."

"Your dad's making you quit our team?"

"He didn't like how I was playing. He thought I was dominating the ball and shooting way too much."

"But that's what Coach Cerrato wants you to do. That's why we're winning."

"My dad says that's not the way to play the game. He says I'm developing bad habits looking for my shot all the time and wants me to pass more. He talked with Coach Russell of the traveling team, who assured him that he emphasizes team ball and finding the open man."

I squeeze the napkin into a ball. What I've feared is here. Isaac's not going to play basketball with us. "We're not going to be any good without you."

"You guys will be okay."

He's trying to make me feel better, but I'm not sure he's giving the real reason he's quitting. Maybe he's quitting because he's tired of wasting his talent with us and wants to play with better players.

He's wrong that we'll be okay without him. We're going to be terrible.

Chapter 18

Sunday morning, I hear ringing, and I'm so deep asleep that I think it's my alarm for school. But when I reach for the phone, Sydney's calling.

"Jackson, we finally got news."

"What?" I sit up in bed.

"Dad's alive. He's going to live. He's badly injured, though. He had to have both legs amputated."

"What?"

"Cut off. Both legs."

"No, I know what it means." I rub my eyes and wonder if this is a bad dream.

"He's alive," Sydney says. "That's what's important. That's what we didn't know about. He's alive."

"Yeah." I'm not sure what to say. Two legs amputated.

How's Mr. Milroy going to get around? How's he going to be able to work?

"Sorry to call you so early," Sydney says, "but I knew you wanted to know right away."

"I'm glad you did. How's Gig doing?"

"I don't know. He's not talking."

"Is it okay if I come over this morning?"

"Yeah, that would be good. He might talk to you."

"How's your mom doing?"

"Okay," Sydney says. "She's so relieved Dad's alive that she's not focused on him coming home in a wheelchair—or at least, she's not talking about it yet."

Sydney seems pretty much in control as she talks. That's a part of her that's always bugged Gig but now seems important. All kinds of things in their family are going to change.

"How are you doing?" I picture Sydney sitting at their kitchen table, the one where Mr. Milroy sat and smoked cigars.

"I'm in shock," she says. "I thought he was dead. I thought we'd lost him. I didn't know how I was going to go forward without him. I felt so lost. Then when I found out he was alive, I was sky high. I know it's going to be hard. I know there's going to be lots of challenges, but he's alive. I still have my dad."

I feel emotional as I listen to her talk. Gig's not talking, and she's putting into words everything she feels. The two of them are so different, yet they're dealing with the same huge thing.

"Thank you," she says.

"For what?"

"For asking, for listening, for caring," she says. "You don't know how much it means."

"It's nothing."

"No, it's not. A lot of friends haven't said anything. They're so afraid of saying the wrong thing that they don't say anything at all. That makes it even harder."

"What time should I come over?"

"How about ten. Gig should be up then."

"Do you think he'll talk to me?"

"I don't know," she says, "but you're our best hope."

After I turn off the phone, my hand is shaking. Mr. Milroy has lost both his legs. I stand up and feel wobbly. How many thousands of steps a day do I take without even thinking about it? Gig's dad isn't going to take those steps ever again.

—

I lie in bed for a while, but I can't sleep. I keep thinking about Gig and Sydney and what they've been through not knowing if their dad was alive or not. No wonder Gig was scared. No wonder he didn't want to talk.

I hear someone moving around in the kitchen, and I get up and find Mom making coffee.

"Why are you up so early?" she asks.

"Sydney called." I tell her about Mr. Milroy.

"Oh, Jackson." She opens up her arms and I move toward her. She gives me a hug, and I feel like a little boy who desperately needs one.

Later, I call Dad, Isaac, and Diego to tell them the news, and everybody reacts the same way: relieved Mr. Milroy is alive but worried about how difficult the adjustment will be, not just for him, but for Gig, Sydney, and their mom.

The sky is gray and threatening, and it looks like it's about to pour when Mom gives me a ride to Gig's house.

"Do you want me to wait here?" she asks as she pulls into the driveway.

"Maybe you should. I don't know if he will see me."

"You go in and check and then let me know."

I ring the bell that I've rung so many times before, but it feels different. I'm going into a completely changed situation.

Sydney answers, and she's dressed in jeans and a tight blue sweater. Her hair's pulled back, and she's put on some makeup. "Thanks for coming," she says.

I step out to wave Mom away, but Sydney says, "Have your mom come in. It would be good for my mom to have someone to talk with."

I go out to tell Mom, and she's embarrassed that she didn't dress better or bring anything. "I should have thought to bring some food."

"Don't worry," I say.

Mrs. Milroy looks scared, but she's eager to talk to Mom as they sit down with their coffee.

Sydney walks me down the hall and points at Gig's door. I remember coming over here last summer to persuade him to go to soccer camp with us.

The warning sign on his door contains some new additions:

STOP. KEEP OUT!

THIS MEANS YOU!

ABSOLUTELY NO TRESPASSING.

YOU'VE BEEN WARNED! YES, THIS MEANS YOU!

BACK AWAY SLOWLY

AND DON'T EVEN THINK OF KNOCKING!

I want to obey the sign and leave him alone. But when I turn, Sydney's at the end of the hall waving me on. I feel caught between the two of them.

I raise my hand to knock but put it down. Maybe I should call. But that doesn't make sense now that I'm right here.

I knock and Gig doesn't answer. I knock again. Nothing.

"Gig, it's me." I stand listening and hear nothing. He doesn't want to see me. "I'm sorry about your dad."

I turn to walk back down the hall, and the door opens. Gig doesn't say anything, but he doesn't have to.

I go into his room and he shuts the door. His room is a complete mess like usual, but it's never looked this bad.

"Sorry," I say again, and he nods. He looks like he's been crying for days. I pull clothes, books, and video game boxes off a chair and sit down. I look at him sitting on his bed, and I've got no idea what to say. What's going on with his dad seems so big and everything else feels so small.

"Blast some zombies." He hands me a controller.

So we fire away together at zombies and do our best to stay alive.

CHAPTER 19

Monday morning, Gig's not at his locker, but I'm not totally surprised. It's going to be hard to come back to school after what he's been through. It's also going to be hard for him to have people asking him questions about his dad.

I wait for Sydney in homeroom, and as soon as she comes in, I go over to her table. "No Gig today?"

"Mom's giving him one more day at home, but she said he's coming tomorrow."

"How's he doing?" I stand as she sits and arranges her books.

"Struggling. That was great you came over to see him, but he said something strange about the assembly."

"What assembly?"

"The Veterans Day assembly. Somehow he thinks there's

a connection between that and Dad getting injured. It's crazy, but he wouldn't say any more about it."

"Take your seats, everybody," Ms. Constantine says. "The bell's going to ring any second."

"I'm glad he's going to be in school. We've got a game tomorrow night. Do you think he'll want to play?"

"Ask him," Sydney says. "It might be good for him."

I take my seat and watch Sydney across the way. She opens up her bag, takes out a tube of ChapStick, and puts some on. For all Gig complains about her, she really does care about him.

In American studies, lots of people have their hands in the air for Mr. Lisicky's question about when the conflict between the Lakota and the United States ended.

"May 7, 1877," one girl reads from her notes. "General Nelson Miles defeated the last band of Miniconju Sioux."

"In 1877, Sitting Bull fled to Canada with some band members to escape the United States government," another girl says.

"Wounded Knee, December 29, 1890," a boy confidently declares. "The Seventh Cavalry, the same unit that was destroyed at Little Bighorn, killed over one hundred and twenty-six men, women, and children. This brought an end to the Indian Wars."

"Anybody else?" Mr. Lisicky walks around the room.

I raise my hand because I think everybody else is way off.

"Jackson."

"The conflict hasn't ended. The Native Americans and the government are still arguing about the Black Hills."

"Exactly," Mr. Lisicky says. "This dispute is not resolved. In 1980, the United States Supreme Court ruled that the Native Americans had the rights to the Black Hills under the 1868 treaty. But instead of ordering the government to return land, the court said the Lakota were entitled to the value of the land at the time, plus interest."

Mr. Lisicky looks around to see if we're paying attention. "But guess what? Even though this tribe has one of the highest poverty rates in the country and the amount of money now exceeds one billion dollars, nobody has taken one cent. The Lakota don't want the money. They want the Black Hills back."

I remember our initial conversation about the different ways the settlers and Native Americans viewed land and owning it.

"Underlying these disputes today between tribes and the government about casinos or sovereignty is the same issue: land." Mr. Lisicky is moving his hands as he talks.

I look down at my notes. Mr. Lisicky connects things that happened a long time ago with what's happening now. He's helped me understand that lots of things don't just occur. They happen because of what happened before.

In FACS, Bossy Boots is writing down tasks for using the washer and dryer on the green sheet for our lab. "Who will put the detergent in?"

"I'll do that," Caleb says.

"Who will sort the items to be washed?"

"I will, Double B." I raise my hand like she's our teacher. It's only towels and washcloths from our food labs, so sorting should be super-easy.

"Who will select the water temperature?"

"I will," Ruby says. I look over at her. She's got her same smooth skin and pretty face, but she looks different now, more far away, like somebody acting.

After the tasks have all been assigned and we're waiting for other groups to finish, she stands next to me. "Did you come to either of *The Music Man* public performances this weekend?" She's wearing her Abercrombie sweatshirt zipped down to the exact inch allowed under the dress code.

"No, I couldn't make it." I don't want to tell her that there's no way I could handle watching her and Chaz make love-eyes at each other. "How did it go?"

"Super. We had a packed house both nights. There were so many people I didn't get a chance to see everybody."

"My best friend got some bad news. I needed to be with him."

"Is he all right? Is everything okay?" Ruby looks directly at me and acts like she's interested. But that's the thing now. I'm not sure if she really cares or if she's acting.

"Things will take a while." I realize I'm being vague, but Gig doesn't want people knowing about his business.

"I hope it all goes well," she says.

"Yeah." I pick up my mechanical pencil and click it a couple of times.

"Are you going to the dance?" Ruby asks.

I can't believe she's asking me. Is she totally unaware how much I wanted to go with her? Are there other guys in the school who she's nice to who felt the same way?

"I don't think so."

"Why not?"

"I don't know who to ask." I look directly at her to see how she'll react.

"Loads of people would like to go with you." She brushes her hair back and turns away. "Just ask someone."

I flip my pencil in my fingers. It's so hard when you think something is one way and it turns out to be completely different.

Just ask someone. Just ask someone. People keep telling me. I'm sick and tired of it. Don't they realize I don't know who to ask?

Chapter 20

I find Gig the next morning at his locker looking around like he's been kidnapped by aliens and dropped off on a distant planet. "Hey." I stand next to him.

He examines his math book like it's a foreign object. "Day One or Day Two?"

"Day Two," I say, referring to the rotation between gym and music.

Gig opens his planner to check his schedule. He's less hyper than usual, and I'm not sure what to say.

"What are you looking at?" he asks.

"Your pretty face."

"Shut up." He slams his locker.

I walk with him even though he's going a different direction from my homeroom.

"Teachers will understand you're behind after missing a couple of days," I say.

"I don't care." Gig walks slowly. "I don't even want to be here. I knew I shouldn't have gone to that assembly last week."

"What do you mean? All you did was stand up."

"I didn't want to make a big deal. I thought if I went about things quietly, things would be okay."

I turn to look at him. "You're not blaming yourself for your dad's accident, are you? You didn't cause it."

He stops in front of the Wall of Heroes display, and we both look up at the picture of him with his dad. They both look so relaxed standing together by their backyard fence, but I can't help focusing on his dad's legs.

"It's not your fault, Gig," I say.

"I feel like I did something to let him down."

"You didn't," I say. "And your dad wouldn't want you feeling that way. He'd get in your face about that."

Gig walks into the sixth-grade section, and I follow.

"Hey, are you going to play in tonight's game?"

"I don't know," Gig says.

"We need you."

We stand outside Gig's homeroom, and it's almost bell

time. I'm going to be late, but it's okay. Some things are more important. I'll tell Ms. Constantine I was helping a friend and hope she'll understand.

"Without Isaac, we need somebody to score points," I say. "You're our best chance. We need you to be the man."

"Maybe." Gig shows the first hint of interest I've seen on him since his dad got hurt.

At lunch, Gig's not talking about his dad, so I don't say anything either. It's up to him whether he wants to bring it up.

"So you've turned your back on us." Gig sits across from Isaac. "Think you're too good for us?"

"Nah, I couldn't stand your stupid jokes." Isaac bites into his turkey sandwich.

"We don't need you." Gig shakes his chocolate milk. "Now we'll at least have a chance to shoot the ball a couple of times a game."

Isaac laughs. Gig doesn't know that shooting the ball so much is the reason Isaac switched to the traveling team.

"What do you think, Diego?" Gig takes a big gulp of milk.

"We're going to miss Isaac. Who's going to score all those points?"

"I will," Gig says. "And you and Jackson will score some, too."

It's good to see Gig back to his overconfident self, but I know him well enough to know it's a cover-up for what's really going on.

"Did you ask someone to the dance?" He turns to me.

"What? No. You're still going?"

"Of course. I'm going to win one of those iPads for being best dancer."

I'm surprised he's playing in the game tonight and going to the dance Friday after the way he was this morning. His mom was right. Being in school and back to his routine has helped.

"Ask somebody." He finishes off his cheeseburger.

"Anybody?"

"Yeah, anybody. Quit being a chicken."

"Okay, I will."

At the next table, Lance Dahlgren is talking loudly. "Basketball players are such babies."

"They're wusses," Cody Bauer joins in.

"They're both," Dahlgren says, and all the hockey players laugh.

Gig turns around. "Shut up. The only reason you play hockey is because you can't play basketball."

"We know how to play," Dahlgren says. "But we don't like girly games."

"At least our jerseys don't look like dresses," Isaac says.

"We've got real jerseys, not the cut-off things you wear that show your puny biceps," Bauer says.

"Basketball requires skills," I say. "We don't just crash into each other."

"Babies." Dahlgren fires a chicken nugget at our table but misses everybody.

"Wusses." Bauer throws a grape that hits Diego in the head.

"That's it." Gig stands up and charges at their table. Isaac, Diego, and I jump up and follow him. The hockey players get up, and all of them except Clark are bigger than me.

"What's going on?" Mr. Tieg, the lunch monitor, hollers. "Back to your seats."

We file back, and for once I'm glad Tieg intervened. I don't want to fight with any of those guys. They'd kill us.

"No more of this hockey versus basketball trash talk," Tieg barks. "The next time this happens, I'll give you all detention for a week."

I look over at the hockey table, where Clark is staring back at me. For winter sports, people have to choose at a young age between hockey and basketball. I can't imagine playing hockey. I'm proud to be a hoopster.

"We're not the same team without Wilkins," Coach Cerrato tells us, stating the obvious during our pregame huddle. "Each of you is going to have to step up to pick up the slack."

I suddenly have a moment of panic. We're playing the Bulls, who are one of the best teams in the league. With Isaac, I'd be confident of a win. Without him, I'm not.

"Starting lineup will be Cerrato, Kennedy, Jimenez, Milroy, and Sportelli," Coach says. "Cerrato, you'll play shooting guard. You'll run the plays that we used to run for Wilkins."

I look over at Gig, whose mouth has dropped open. There's no way Tony can run Isaac's plays and get the points he did.

"Go, Red on three," Coach says. "One, two, three."

"Go, Red." There's a hesitancy I haven't heard before.

We form a circle for the opening tip, and I shake hands with my opponent. He's taller than I am, weighs more, and has pickle breath. Diego's guy is taller, too. We're going to have our hands full.

They control the ball, and I hurry back on defense. Pickle Breath cuts to the hoop, and I weave around players to stay with him. An outside shot goes up, and I box out, and Diego pushes in for the rebound. He passes to Gig, who brings the ball up and checks the play with Coach.

"One." Gig holds up his index finger.

Diego sets a screen and Tony slides off it. Gig delivers the pass and Tony shoots, but the shot is way off. It doesn't even hit iron, and the air ball sails out of bounds.

"That's okay, Cerrato." Coach claps. "Keep looking for your shot."

I turn to Gig, who's frowning. This could be a disaster. It also bugs me the way Coach keeps saying Cerrato for Tony. It's weird when it's his son and it's both their last names.

On our next possession, Tony puts up another wild shot, and on the third he travels. Finally on the fourth possession, Gig drives into the lane, fakes a pass, and puts in a tough hook shot.

"Good move, Gig," I say and look over at Coach.

"Run the plays," he says.

At halftime, we're down twenty-one to nine when Gig, Diego, and I step out for a drink of water.

"We only have nine points," Gig says.

"Isaac used to get that many in a quarter." I wipe my face on my jersey.

"We need him," Diego adds.

"He's gone," Gig says. "We've got to figure how to play without him, but Tony shooting all the time isn't working. Be ready, I'm going to start driving."

In the third quarter, Tony's sitting out, and Gig takes over. He fakes left, drives right, and tosses up a bank shot for two points. He splits two defenders, draws another one, and flips me a pass for an easy layup. He feeds Diego on a two on one break with a no-look pass, and we close the deficit to eight.

Underneath the basket, Diego and I are going hard after every loose ball and rebound. Diego seems to anticipate where the shot will come off the rim, and he's strong enough to get past his guy for the ball. I score another couple of baskets off good feeds from Gig. G-Man, Quinn, and Dad cheer from the sideline, and at the end of the quarter, we're within five.

In the fourth quarter, Coach puts Tony back in and takes Gig out, which makes no sense. Sam runs the point, and Coach keeps calling play number one for Tony, who doesn't remind anyone of Isaac. We lose by thirteen, but it doesn't even feel that close.

As I'm taking off my shoes, I sit between Gig and Diego.

"I'm not running that stupid play for Tony on Saturday," Gig says. "Without Isaac, it's crazy."

"We'll do what we did in the third quarter," I say. "You drive and shoot or pass to me or Diego."

"Remember, I'm not going to be there Saturday," Diego says.

"You've got to be for us to have a chance," Gig says.

"Ask your uncle if you can miss one day," I say. "Just one day. We're desperate."

CHAPTER 21

I go straight to homeroom Wednesday morning, and I'm one of the first students there. "I'm early today, Ms. Constantine."

"That's better." She adjusts her necklace of green glass beads. She was sympathetic yesterday when I explained why I was late.

I set my books and planner on the table and sit down. But I stand up right away and go to the window to look out. A cold rain's falling and it's miserable out. I walk back to my table and sit down.

I'm going to do it today. I'm going to ask someone to the dance. My hands are sweaty as I squeeze them together. There are only three kids here, and I'm not used to being so early for homeroom.

I get up and go to the hall to get a drink. When I'm done, I wipe my mouth on my sleeve and see Sydney and Kelsey coming down the hall together. They stop and talk, and then Kelsey waves good-bye and turns in another direction.

"Hey," I say to Sydney.

"Good morning, Jackson."

"Can I ask you a question?"

"Sure." Sydney's wearing jeans and a purple Longview sweatshirt.

"Are you going to the dance on Friday?"

"No." She shakes her head.

"Do you want to go with me?"

"I'd love to." Sydney smiles wide and so do I. I can't believe it's that easy. I asked and she said yes. I'm going to the dance. I'm tempted to ask again to double-check, but that would sound like I don't believe it.

"It will be fun." I say the same dumb thing that everybody has been telling me.

"It definitely will." Sydney shifts her books.

We both stand there, and I'm not sure what to say. I've been so focused on asking somebody that I forgot about the part that comes afterward. Should I say more about the dance? Ask about her dad?

"I heard you guys had a tough loss last night," Sydney says, giving me something easy to talk about.

"Yeah, our first of the year." I describe the game and ask how her team is doing.

"We've won two and lost one. We play tonight."

Sydney and I walk into homeroom together, and I feel great knowing I'm going to the dance with her. I'm not going to be the only one of my friends left behind.

"See you later," Sydney says as she sets her books down.

"Yeah." I take my seat and feel like there should be some dramatic announcement by Ms. Constantine that I'm going to the dance. Not really, but I want people to know I'm going with Sydney.

I've still got one person to deal with and that's Gig. I don't know how he'll react.

In gym, even Mr. Tieg decides it's too cold out and lets us play kickball inside.

"Finally, something fun." I stand behind Diego as we wait our turns to kick.

Tieg goes through the rules, including his special one that any kick that hits the wall or the bleachers in the air is an automatic out.

"I'm going to the dance," I tell Diego.

"With who?"

"Sydney."

"Awesome," he says.

Trenton kicks a soft fly that the other team catches for the first out.

"Did you ask your uncle about Saturday?" I ask.

"I've got to work." Diego moves behind home plate.

"What time do you start?"

"Seven in the morning." He concentrates as Tieg rolls a fastball. Diego blasts it between third base and shortstop and races around to second base.

I survey the field and decide where I want to place it.

Tieg rolls a bouncer, and I drill it right down the third baseline.

"Fair ball," Tieg calls as I zoom to first, make the turn, and arrive at second with a stand-up double. This is how gym should be.

"Good kick." Diego claps from the side after scoring the first run of the game.

I stand on the base and wait for somebody to bring me in. All of a sudden, an idea flashes into my mind about how I might be able to get Diego to play with us Saturday.

—

At lunch, I slide my tray behind Gig as we go through the line. He chooses spaghetti and cheesy garlic bread, and I do, too.

"I finally asked someone to the dance, and she said yes," I say casually.

"Who is it?" Gig picks out a banana.

"Somebody you know." I grab a tangerine.

"Who?"

"Sydney."

He stops and turns around. "Out of everybody in the school you chose Squid Face?"

"Yeah."

"Because you felt sorry for her?"

"No, I am sorry about what she's going through and what you're going through, but that's not the reason."

"Keep moving." Speros pushes behind me.

"You said to ask anyone," I say.

Gig picks up his tray and shakes his head. "I never thought you'd ask her. You're not going to win any prizes. She can't dance."

"That's okay." I punch in my lunch code.

"She'll be trouble," he says. "You wait and see."

“Pull up those pants, Milroy. No sagging in school,” Tieg says in his drill-sergeant voice.

Gig shifts his tray to one hand and yanks his pants up with the other.

When we sit down with Isaac, I give him the news about Sydney, and he's glad. He likes her, too. It's only Gig who doesn't want me going with Sydney. Too bad. He said ask anybody. He didn't rule out his sister.

Wednesday night I get Dad to drop me off at school to watch the girls' basketball game while he and Quinn go to Target.

“I'll pick you up in an hour,” he says.

I walk into school, and it feels strange to be going to a girls' game. I follow the cheers to the gym, where the game has already started. It's tied at four, and Sydney's bringing the ball up the court. She passes to Kelsey, who sends it back. Sydney dribbles twice, stops and draws the defender. She shuffles a pass to Kelsey, who scores an easy layup.

Sydney hurries back on defense, and I watch her move around the court in her green jersey, with her ponytail flapping side to side. She looks good. She looks confident.

Kelsey knocks a pass out of bounds that bounces my way.

I grab it and hand it to the ref. Sydney sees me and smiles. She didn't expect me to show up and that makes being here even better.

I'm so glad I'm going to the dance with her. The answer of who to ask wasn't so difficult. Sydney was right in front of me the whole time.

CHAPTER 22

After I look up a couple of facts on the Mayan civilization for Spanish class, I click my e-mail and see something I don't recognize: FutureMe.org. I open the message.

Warning to FutureMe,

Stay tight with Diego, Isaac, and Gig. Don't let anyone break up the group. Don't you do anything to break up the group. Do everything you can to keep things together.

Friends are even more important in middle school. Am I right?

Have you been beat up at Longview? Are the bullies as mean as you thought?

Is the homework bad? Are the teachers mean?

Have you gotten taller? Stronger?

You should go look at a picture of yourself from fifth grade to see how much you've changed.

Do you miss elementary school one tiny bit or are you glad to be gone?

Are the girls hot? Do you have a girlfriend yet? What's her name?

You rock,
Your fifth-grade self

P.S. Have you ever seen that ghost again?

Wow. It's the message I sent to myself six months ago from that website where you send e-mails to yourself in the future.

I reread the message thinking about my warning to myself and answering my questions. Yes, I'm still tight with Diego, Isaac, and Gig. We're tight even though Isaac's playing on the traveling team, and, yes, friends are even more important in middle school than I thought. I've done a lot to keep things together this year, but I asked Sydney to the dance even though I knew Gig wouldn't like it.

No, I haven't been beat up, but there are bullies, like

Wolfram and Steck, and sixth graders always need to be careful.

Yes, the homework's hard, and, yes, teachers like Tieg and Tedesco are mean, but others like Lisicky, Tremont, and Mrs. Randall are nice.

Yes, I am taller and stronger, and I'll try to find a picture from fifth grade to see how much I've changed. Fifth grade seems so long ago.

I miss recess and Principal Maroney from Cranston, but I'm glad to be a middle schooler. I'm glad to be at Longview.

Yes, lots of girls are hot, and I do have someone I'm going to the dance with. I guess that makes her a girlfriend. And, yes, fifth-grade self, you'll recognize the name. She's someone you know: Sydney Milroy.

No, I haven't seen the ghost. That's probably something I made up back when I was a scared fifth grader on my middle school visit. Now, Longview feels so familiar that it's hard to imagine ghosts here.

I reread the message one more time, and I'm glad I sent it. My fifth-grade self feels like an old friend who I'm glad to hear from. He also feels like he's not just back in the past. He's inside me. My fifth-grade self is part of my sixth-grade self.

My phone rings, and it's Mom with more reminders of everything we've got to do tomorrow and Friday to get ready for the wedding.

"I've got something on Friday night," I say.

"What?"

"I'm going to the school dance."

"Oh, Jackson, a dance. How are we going to fit everything in? You're going to have to prepare everything tomorrow then." Mom's talking a mile a minute. "Who are you going with?"

"Sydney."

"Oh, that's nice of you to ask her. Her mom will be pleased."

I listen while Mom keeps talking. I didn't ask Sydney to be nice. I asked her because I want to go with her.

Dad walks into the living room after I'm done with my call. I'd already told him earlier about going to the dance with Sydney, and he's happy for me.

"Quinn, come on in here and sit down. I've got a surprise."

Quinn races in and looks at me, but I shrug my shoulders. Dad doesn't have anything in his hands, and I don't see any boxes or anything.

"I've given this a lot of thought," he says.

I watch his face. I hope *he's* not getting ready to announce he's getting married.

"I didn't see how it was possible, but your grandfather stepped up to make it work because he knows how important this is to you."

Quinn looks to me again, but I don't have any idea what Dad is talking about.

"Are you ready?" he asks.

"Yes! Yes!" Quinn says. "What is it?"

Dad takes out his phone and calls someone. "They're ready."

I look to Dad, but he's not giving anything away. There's a sound at the door and it opens.

A big brown dog walks through with G-Man holding the leash.

Quinn leaps from the couch and hugs the dog around the neck. The dog's so gentle that he doesn't flinch or pull away.

"It's our dog?" I go over to pet it, and big brown eyes look up softly at me.

"It is now." Dad stands up.

"But who's going to take care of it when we're at Mom's and you're working?"

“I volunteered,” G-Man says. “I knew how much Quinn wanted a dog, and I thought you’d enjoy it, too. Then Scout needed a good home, and I thought we could provide that. He’s a smart dog. He’s better behaved than a lot of adults I know.”

“Where did he come from?”

“My neighbors adopted a girl who’s allergic to dogs,” G-Man says. “I’ve known Scout for years, and I knew two boys who needed a dog.”

Quinn scratches Scout behind the ears. “Thank you,” he says. “Thank you.”

Scout rolls over on his back, and Quinn and I rub his belly. I see Dad turn to G-Man and smile.

We’ve finally got our dog. We’ve got Scout.

CHAPTER 23

Thursday after school, I've got someone I need to send a message to.

Hey Man,

How's seventh grade going? How are your classes? Do you have some with Gig? Isaac? Diego?

You guys are still tight, right? Remember, stay together no matter what happens. By staying together, you stay strong.

How's Sydney? Are you still going out with her? How's Mr. Milroy doing now that he's home?

How did football go? Was Mr. Amodt a good coach? How about Tieg in basketball? I'm worried about him and how tough he is.

Remember, even if you and your friends do different

things, you can still stay together. Be yourself. You're awesome.

Are you even cooler than you used to be? I thought so.

Have fun,

Your sixth-grade self

I'm already looking forward to receiving that message next year to see how things are going.

Basketball practice is at Cranston, my old elementary school. Inside, everything feels smaller and more cramped after being at Longview. Outside the office, pictures of the fifth-grade graduating classes are lined up, and I find ours from last year.

In the picture, I'm standing with Gig, Isaac, and Diego, and we're all laughing—probably at something Gig said. I look closely at myself and can't believe I looked like that less than six months ago. I look about two years younger.

Gig, Diego, and Isaac look a lot younger, too. I find Sydney, who's standing next to Kelsey. She always seemed more mature than us in fifth grade, but she's changed, too. In the picture, she looks younger than the girl I'm taking to the dance.

As I walk down to the gym, I think about Longview. School's settled into a routine of assignments, homework, and quizzes. But the stuff outside of school like Isaac switching to the traveling team, Mr. Milroy getting injured, or asking Sydney to the dance feels huge. I don't notice day-to-day changes, but when I think back to fifth grade, a lot has changed.

Tony's on the court practicing shooting, and Gig's in a discussion with Coach Cerrato. I go over to hear what they're talking about while I take my sweatshirt off.

"If I drive, I can create scoring chances for Diego and Jackson or I can shoot myself," Gig says.

"What happens if they pack everything into the paint?"

"I can kick it back out to Tony or Sam. They should have wide-open shots."

Coach sees me listening. "What do you think, Kennedy?"

"I think Gig's right. The offense was better when he ran it that way."

"I'll think about it," Coach says.

I take my Nikes out of my gym bag and sit down to put them on.

"Have you changed your mind yet?" Gig stands next to me.

"About what?"

"Going to the dance with Barf Breath."

I shake my head at him.

"Don't say I didn't warn you." Gig picks up a ball and goes out to shoot with Tony. It's almost like he's going through the motions of giving me a hard time about Sydney, but he's not really angry. I've seen him angry enough to know what that looks like.

Maybe he's even glad she's going. Maybe he looks out for her more than he pretends.

Diego, Sam, Trenton, and Noah file in, and Coach blows his whistle.

"Let's start out with our lay-up lines."

I stand up and think about the different coaches I've had this year and the different ways they started practice. With Coach Wilkins, Isaac's dad, in baseball we always started with stretching. Same with Coach Derek at soccer camp. Same with Coach Martineau and Coach Tanglen in football. Coach Cerrato never has us stretch. It's not like we love stretching, but something is missing.

He coached us poorly in the last game, too, letting Tony shoot so much. Like the rest of us, he was used to Isaac being the best player in the league and taking over. But now that we don't have him, Gig's right. We've got to do something different.

Coach has us run our regular plays and keeps Tony at shooting guard even though he's still struggling with his shot. Those plays worked when Isaac was making the shots, but they don't now.

At the end, we split up into teams to go four on four, but we're one short, so Coach plays with Tony, Noah, and Sam. I'm with Gig, Diego, and Trenton, and Gig pulls me aside before we start.

"I'm driving," he says. "Be ready to take your best shot."

On the floor, Gig's a whirligig, just like his nickname, twisting and turning and slicing through small spaces. He puts up shots and scores and gets the ball to me and Diego when we're open.

Coach is crowding the hoop, so I step out on the baseline, my favorite spot, to give myself more room. Gig drives and passes to me, and I hit the wide-open shot.

Underneath the hoop, Diego battles for position and grabs rebounds even when he's going up against Coach. We absolutely have to have him Saturday to have any chance against the Kings.

At the end of practice, I grab him.

"What's your uncle's phone number?"

"Which uncle?" he asks.

"The one you work with on Saturdays."

"Why?"

"Just give it to me. I've got an idea."

The Dance. The Dance. The Dance. Kids keep talking about it Friday at school. I try to pay attention to my teachers, but it's too hard. I'm thinking about the dance, too, and I'm excited I'm going with Sydney.

But I also notice the kids who aren't going. I thought I was going to be one of them last week. I would have pretended I didn't care, but with all my friends going, it would have been hard. It feels way better to be a part of it.

In lab groups in FACS, Ruby's chattering on about Chaz again, and she still can't believe he asked her. It's hard for me to believe I ever thought she'd go with me.

"Chaz says I'll be perfect for the ghost in the spring," she says.

"What ghost?"

"Every year, when the fifth graders visit Longview, the

drama students choose one person to be the ghost of the girl with long blonde hair. Didn't you ever hear that story about the girl who dropped dead at her locker?"

I shake my head. I'm not going to tell Ruby that when I saw the ghost last spring, I thought it was real and told Gig about it. "I don't think that's right," I say.

"Why not?"

"Fifth graders are scared enough on their middle school visit. You shouldn't add to it."

"I didn't think about it like that," Ruby says. "I was excited to wear the wig and put on the dress when Chaz said I'd make a good ghost."

"You would, but I still don't like the idea." I move around to the other side of the table.

"I'll think about it," she says.

"Who's spraying the baking pan?" Bossy Boots asks.

"I am, Double B." I pick up the can.

Ruby puts her hands on her hips and imitates the way Bossy Boots moves, and I laugh. Maybe we can still be friends, friends in a different way. I still like being around her in FACS, and she does an excellent imitation of Bossy Boots, but I don't want to go to the dance with Ruby anymore. I want to go with Sydney.

—

Friday night, Dad's working and Mom and Ted are taking care of last-minute wedding preparations, so G-Man volunteers to drive Sydney and me to the dance. He's got another passenger in the front seat when he picks me up: Scout.

"He's a great car dog," G-Man says. "He sits quietly and watches traffic. I can't wait until it's warm and I can roll down the windows for him."

I scratch Scout behind the ears, and I'm so glad Sydney is Sydney. Some girls wouldn't want to be picked up by G-Man and a dog, but she'll be fine with it. She and G-Man became friends when she was on our baseball team and he practiced the double play with us.

"I'm glad you're going with Sydney," G-Man says. "She's pretty impressive."

"Thanks." Scout leans in and I rub his head.

When I ring the doorbell, Gig answers, which he hardly ever does. "Sure you don't want to bail out?" He's wearing dark pants, a dark shirt, and a dark jacket.

"You look sharp."

"I've got to if we're going to be best dancers."

"Is Sydney ready?"

"Almost. You know how long it takes girls."

He leads me up to the kitchen and I greet his mom.

"You look great, Jackson," she says.

"Thanks, you do, too." As soon as I say it, I realize it doesn't sound right. I meant she looks a lot better than last time I saw her.

"I'm so happy you're all going," she says, and I realize how hard it would have been for her if Gig had gone and Sydney hadn't.

When Sydney comes out, she looks beautiful. She's smiling shyly, and her hair is shiny. She's wearing a long silver dress that shimmers as she moves. Her cheeks are flushed and her eyelashes darkened. She doesn't look at all like that tough second baseman I played baseball with in the spring.

The decorating committee has transformed the gym at Longview. Purple streamers hang down, soft lighting circles the floor, and it feels more like a dance club and less like a gym.

The floor is packed, and Sydney and I end up hanging out with Kelsey and Diego and Isaac and Vanessa. Gig's running around with Zoe and dancing every single dance as hard as he can.

I'm not a big dancer and neither is Sydney, so we get

plenty of time to talk. She asks about my mom, and I tell her all about the wedding, which I haven't been talking about much.

"How do you feel about it?" she asks.

"Fine," I say. "It makes sense for them to get married, but I don't want her to force the perfect-family stuff. It will take time to work things out."

We talk about her dad and she says he's recovering steadily. "He's going to be fitted for prostheses."

"What?"

"Artificial legs. They've gotten so much better that he's going to be able to move around with them. It's going to require months of physical therapy, but he's going to do it. He's going to go through rehabilitation, and then he'll be back home."

Talking to Sydney is easy, like talking to someone I've known a long time, not someone new. She's smart and a good listener, and I love seeing her all dressed up. I also love it that she can bump around to grab a rebound or get dirty turning a double play. I love that combination in her.

"Come on. Let's dance." Syd pulls my hand, and we go out for a slow dance.

I put my hands on her hips, and she wraps her arms

around me. I smell her perfume and it's exciting to be so close.

We rock back and forth together, and I'm so happy to be here with her.

At the end of the dance, I look into her green eyes, and before I can even think, she leans in and our lips meet for our first kiss, my first kiss.

It's wet and smooshy and tastes surprisingly good.

Chapter 24

Saturday morning, I've got my plan set up, and Mom's agreed since my clothes and shoes for the wedding are all ready. Dad picks me up and looks tired after another late night at the restaurant. He comes in to wish Ted and Mom congratulations on their big day, and I grab the directions I printed and my gym bag.

Dad drives back along Border Parkway and asks me questions about the dance and who was there. I tell him about it and also read the MapQuest directions, which take us toward Echo Park. We wind around curvy streets in a neighborhood I don't know. Finally, we pull up in front of a two-story house with a ginormous green Dumpster in the street. Big oak trees that have lost their leaves surround the house.

"This is it." I open my door and grab my bag. Dad and I

walk past piles of gray shingles as nail guns pound out a steady beat.

"You must be Jackson." A big man extends his hand. "I'm Felipe."

"Hi." I shake his firm grip that gobbles up my hand.

Felipe thanks Dad for bringing me over and asks Dad to leave my bag on the sidewalk so he can put it in his truck.

"*¿Hablas español?*" Felipe asks me.

"*Poquito.*" I hold up my thumb and finger close together to indicate a little.

"That's good," Felipe says. "Some of the crew don't speak much English."

I pull on my sweatshirt hood and zip up my coat. It's sunny this morning, but there's a chill in the air.

"Two hours," Felipe says. "That's our deal. You work two hours with Diego, and he gets to come to the game."

"Yep." I pull on my work gloves.

"Is he any good?"

"Yeah, we really need him."

"Diego," Felipe calls, and Diego comes around from the back of the house.

"I still don't believe you're doing this." Diego wears an old Astros baseball hat with his work clothes.

"Show Jackson what to do." Felipe moves a ladder. "Let's get to work."

So Diego and I load shingles, broken boards, rusted-out gutters, and roofing paper into a wheelbarrow and push it around to the front, into the street, and up a ramp to the Dumpster.

"We'll fill this all up," Diego says, "so pack it tight."

I tip the wheelbarrow and kick stuff with my boots.

"Watch out for nails," Diego says.

We pick up load after load and I lose track of time. I watch Diego for a signal that we get to take a break, but that doesn't happen. Everybody keeps working hard, and the guys on the roof nail row after row of new shingles.

Our pile in the Dumpster grows and grows, and two guys who speak Spanish come down to close the gate. After that, Diego shows me how to stack the shingles so we can toss them over the side in bunches. I never knew shingles were so heavy, and I can't believe Diego works like this every Saturday.

When our Dumpster is almost full, Diego and I climb up on top to pack it down to create more space. I tromp down on an old pallet and crush shingles, broken wood, and roofing paper. I stand on the pallet to survey the full Dumpster and see how much work we've done.

—

"We're going to run you into the ground," Steve Stein says as we line up for our game against the Kings.

"Shut up," Gig says.

"Where's Isaac? I heard he deserted you," Cole Gunderson joins in. "You guys aren't so confident now."

"Kings rule," Stein says.

"Jets fly high," Gig shoots back.

Corbin Tilson, their huge center, easily wins the tip, and Stein brings the ball up.

Diego bangs with Tilson and gets whistled for a quick foul.

"Play smart," I say. "We need you out there." I don't want him fouling out after doing that work to get him here.

Gunderson fakes a shot and drives around me for the first basket.

"Don't fall for the fake," Coach calls.

On offense, we run play number one, and Tony makes a hoop, which is good and bad. Good because it ties the game, but bad because it encourages Coach to stay with the old offense.

On defense, Stein passes to Tilson, and Diego slides over

to stop the drive. Tilson turns to flip up a hook shot, and I stick my hand out to block it.

"Good work." Coach claps.

At the end of the first quarter, we're down twelve to five, and at halftime we're down twenty to thirteen. Diego and I walk to the water fountain together. "Good defense on Tilson," I say.

"He's a monster. Thanks for the help." He slaps my hand. We're working together on the court like we did this morning when we filled the Dumpster.

When we get back, Coach surprises us with a change in strategy.

"Milroy's going to penetrate and look for open shooters. Cerrato, Hauser, and Kennedy, set up in your favorite spots, and when Milroy finds you, take your best shot."

I bound out onto the floor. Gig running the offense sounds a lot more fun than watching Tony miss shots.

Tilson's so big and strong that to keep out of his way I line up on the baseline, as I did in practice. On Gig's first drive he passes to me, but I'm covered, so I swing it back to Noah. He hits the shot and we cut it to five.

After the way we got pushed around in the first half, it's

surprising to be so close and we turn up the pressure at the other end. I slap down and knock the ball out of Gunderson's hands. Gig picks up the loose ball and goes right into the teeth of the defense and draws a foul on Tilson.

At the end of the third quarter, we've pulled within three, and Gunderson and Stein are looking nervous.

"Let's go, Jets," calls a familiar voice on the other side of the court. It's Isaac, who is here with Quincy and Dante. They must have come straight from their traveling-team practice to cheer us on.

The game stays tight through the fourth quarter. Gunderson and Stein each hit long shots, and Tilson puts back a miss. But Gig keeps spinning and driving and finding space, and with one minute left we've pulled within one.

Stein brings the ball down and passes to Gunderson.

"Trap him," Isaac yells.

Gig flies down with his hands up, and Gunderson lofts a pass back to Stein. Out of nowhere, Diego taps the ball to Trenton, who wraps it up like a baby.

"Time out. Time out," I holler before anybody can steal it from him.

"Time out, Red," the ref calls. "Twenty-two seconds left."

Coach picks play number one for Tony to take the last

shot, and I can't believe it. That didn't work in the first half, so why would we go back to it now with the game on the line?

"Team on three," Coach says. "One, two, three."

"TEAM!" we shout.

As we file back onto the court, Gig grabs Diego and me.

"Be ready," he says. "I'm taking over."

Trenton passes the ball to Gig, who races up the floor.

"One, one, one," Coach is calling the play, but Gig ignores him.

I run behind Trenton, trying to get free of Gunderson. Gig drives to the hoop and forces a pass to Diego. Tilson gets his hand on it and knocks the ball out of bounds.

"Red ball." The ref looks over to the scorekeeper. "Nine seconds left."

"Inbounds play two," Coach shouts.

Gig holds up two fingers and slaps the ball to signal he's ready to throw it in. I run down from my spot on the free throw line, but Gunderson sticks to me like glue. Underneath the hoop, Tilson is blanketing Diego. Nobody's open and we're out of time-outs.

Gig fires the pass right at Tilson's back, and the ball bounces off him. Gig races to grab it. Gunderson rushes over to defend him, and I slide to the baseline. Gig zings me a pass.

I don't even think. I catch and shoot, and as soon as the ball leaves my hand, it feels good. I watch the ball drop through the net. We won! We won!

Everybody on our team grabs me. Isaac rushes onto the court and gives me a bear hug. We did it. We beat the Kings, even without Isaac, our star. We did it on our own.

I'm still excited about the game as I stand with Quinn, Heather, and Haley, watching Mom and Ted get married. Mom's wearing a long green dress, and Ted's got on a brown suit with one of those ties with a hint of orange he liked so much. I still like my green and blue one better.

I look around the church and see Mom's brother and sister, my cousins, and Liz and Jeff, whose house we stayed in last year when they were in Italy. Some of Mom's work friends are here, too.

Ted's got more family, including his mother, who uses a walker. He's also got a bunch of golf buddies and people from his work.

I try to concentrate on the words being said, but I keep flashing back to my game-winning shot. If Isaac was still on the team, he'd have taken it. Without him, I had to be ready to take the shot.

"I now pronounce you husband and wife." I'm brought back to what's in front of me, and Mom looks into Ted's eyes and they kiss. They both look really happy and all of us clap.

While the photographer is taking pictures, I stand next to Heather, who's wearing a new green dress that goes with Mom's but isn't identical.

"I'm happy for them," she says.

"Me, too." And I really am. I didn't like Ted at first, but he's turned out to be okay, and Mom and he are nuts about each other. Ted knows I've got my own dad, and he's not trying quite so hard, which actually makes it easier.

I ask Heather what's new with her, and she tells me about deciding between another wilderness canoe trip or backpacking in the Rocky Mountains this summer.

"I love canoeing," she says, "but Dad thinks I should try the backpacking at least once."

"What do you want to do?" I ask.

"Go canoeing."

"Then do it," I say. "Do what you love."

Heather heard Mom talking about the dance, so she asks me about it, and I tell her about Sydney and how Gig and

Zoe won iPads for being the best dancers, and Gig was so excited.

"That's excellent. Tell me more about Sydney."

And so I do, and as I talk, I realize Heather reminds me a little of Syd. She's not the athlete Syd is, but she's smart and confident. She's going to be a good stepsister.

In the corner, Quinn, the ring bearer, is having his picture taken with Haley, the flower girl. She's going to be fine, too.

This is going to work out better than I thought.

CHAPTER 25

Tuesday, at school, Mr. Amodt carries a stack of old hard-cover books to our table for READ Club. "You're going to take these apart. That's one way to find out how they're made."

"We really get to cut them apart?" Gig asks.

"Yes, they've been taken out of circulation and would be discarded. This way, we'll learn something."

"Cool," Diego says.

Mr. Amodt hands me an old blue book about Paul Revere. I remember him from when we talked about the Revolutionary War in Mr. Lisicky's class. I open it up and feel a little bad for the book. It's like getting cut from a team. Newer and better books have come along and knocked it off.

"You're not supposed to read it," Isaac says.

"I know. I can't help it."

Mr. Amodt demonstrates how to cut along the inside of the spine with an X-ACTO knife and pull the end papers from the corners.

"I love destroying things," Gig says.

I peel the end papers off and separate the hard cover from the pages.

"The pages are grouped in signatures," Mr. Amodt says. "Now, cut the string that holds them together."

I do and the pages fall apart. I look across the room at Sydney, who's cutting carefully beside Kelsey. I keep my eyes on her hoping she'll look up. Finally she does, like she can read my mind.

I smile, and her smile beams back across the room.

"One day until Thanksgiving break," Isaac says.

"I can't wait," Diego says.

"I can't wait for pumpkin and pecan pie." Gig rips his pages apart.

"Me, too." I snip signatures and think about all that's happened. Gig, Isaac, Diego, and I are together. Even with Isaac on another team, we're still together. Sydney and I are going out. Mr. Milroy's coming home from Afghanistan. Ted and Mom are married, and Scout's joined us at Dad's.

I pull the string from the last signature. I've got loads to be thankful for this Thanksgiving.

"Did you know it's only ten weeks until pitchers and catchers report to spring training?" Gig says.

"That's all?"

"Baseball will be here before you know it."

I'm excited. Gig knows baseball's my favorite sport.

"Who's going to play on the team with me this year?" he asks.

"I'm in for sure," I say.

"Me, too." Isaac holds up his hand.

"Me, three," Diego says.

"No traveling team?" Gig asks Diego.

"No, I want to play with you guys."

"Together," Gig says and presses his palm against mine. I press mine against Diego's, and he presses Isaac's, who presses back with Gig to complete the circle.

"Together!" we all say.

At Dad's house, I sit at the computer after finishing my homework, and Scout lies sleeping at my feet. I've got one more message to send off to the future.

Hey Jackson,

It's me, Jackson, your younger self, your sixth-grade self. What's up? Where are you living? What are you doing?

You went to college, right? Where? How is it? You'd be a senior now. Are you on track to graduate? Do you have a job?

Do you have a girlfriend? What's her name? Do you still see Sydney?

How are Gig, Diego, and Isaac? What are they doing? Are you still staying together after all these years? You should call each of them right now. Better yet, get on a video chat together.

What other cool technologies do you have now? Do you have personal transporters? Robots to do all your work? Time machines?

How are Mom, Dad, Ted, Quinn, Heather, and Haley? What are they doing? Is G-Man still going strong? Still wearing ridiculous swim trunks? How about Scout?

I bet you're a pretty cool adult. You always had coolness. If they have invented time travel, come back

for a visit. I'd really like to meet you and see how we turned out.

You and me,
Jackson

I click the button to send the message ten years into the future. I already know some of the answers to my questions. I am going to college, and I will see Sydney one way or another. I don't know the answers to everything else, but I know one thing for sure: Gig, Isaac, Diego, and I are staying together as friends for good.

Acknowledgments

This fourth book in the **4 for 4** series would not have been possible without the support and assistance of many people. Thank you all for sharing your thoughts and feedback with me.

Particular thanks to the teachers and students at Valley Middle School for welcoming me and sharing their stories. Thank you also to the other middle schools I visited as I was working on this book. I learned so much from you.

Thanks to Liz Szabla, Jean Feiwel, Elizabeth Fithian, Rich Deas, Lizzy Mason, Dave Barrett, Gabrielle Danchick, and everybody at Feiwel and Friends. I am so pleased to work together.

Thanks to my agent Andrea Cascardi, who knows how to run a team, and the KTM writers who stay calm with the game on the line.

Thanks to Jay Patrikios and Matt Sly for their great website: www.futureme.org. Yes, it's real.

Thanks to Principal Sally Soliday and everyone at Echo Park Elementary School, particularly Dan Dudley and Kim Coleman and their impressive students for their excellent ideas.

Thanks to Principal Kim Hill and everyone at Flynn Elementary School, particularly Cheryl Lawrence and Matt Wigdahl and their students for their thoughtful suggestions.

And above all, my deepest thanks to Fiona McCrae, who was there from word one. Love.

Thank you for reading this FEIWEL AND FRIENDS book.

The Friends who made

TAKE YOUR BEST SHOT

possible are:

Jean Feiwel
publisher

Liz Szabla
editor-in-chief

Rich Deas
creative director

Elizabeth Fithian
marketing director

Holly West
assistant to the publisher

Dave Barrett
managing editor

Nicole Liebowitz Moulaison
production manager

Lauren Burniac
associate editor

Ksenia Winnicki
publishing associate

Anna Roberto
editorial assistant

Kathleen Breitenfeld
designer

Find out more about our authors and artists
and our future publishing at mackids.com.

OUR BOOKS ARE FRIENDS FOR LIFE